Hiding Behind The Couch

To Be Sure

by
Debbie McGowan

Beaten Track
www.beatentrackpublishing.com

To Be Sure

First published 2017 by Beaten Track Publishing
Copyright © 2017, 2018 Debbie McGowan

All rights reserved.

ISBN: 978 1 78645 165 1

Beaten Track Publishing,
Burscough. Lancashire.
www.beatentrackpublishing.com

Contents

Acknowledgements

I could go on, go on, go on, go on...like Mrs. Doyle, except that's the wrong part of Ireland, although tea-drinking is a national pastime of both fair isles (Ireland/UK), but I digress and this acknowledgements section is already a bit on the long side.

First, a general (but no less heartfelt) thanks to all of the authors who took up the challenge of writing a story for the 'SAGA' anthology. You are brilliant and have made it possible for me to wake up every day loving my work. Thank you so much for trusting me to look after your stories.

Mighty thanks to my fabulous (and abundant) beta-readers: Al-pha-reader Stewart (in the past, present and future...perfect), A.M. Leibowitz (you have no idea how excited I get at a GDoc comments notification), Dee Aditya, Lynn Michaels and Nige the Pige (I fancied a change).

Epic thanks also to my proofreader extraordinaire, Jor Barrie. Sometimes, when the mindfulness wobbles, I reminisce how we reached this point; I'm so happy we did.

And even though she's a total wind-up merchant...

> **Andrea:** Oh, by the way, To Be Sure...can I be honest with you?
>
> **Deb:** (expecting the worst, rationalising...she likes all the others, I can take the hit...big breath...it'll be OK...) Go on.

Andrea: I read it in the middle of the night. When I went back to sleep afterwards, I dreamed there would be a part two. That was intuition, not wishful thinking, right?

Deb: LMAO. You bugger.

Mate, I've said it before, but I can't say it often enough. Thank you so much for everything.

So...Ellie character special next, then, yes?

Lastly, thanks to all those who freely share their ideas online, especially 'Blackkat' for sharing their naming ceremony – it was excellent inspiration.

Author's Note

In the North of Ireland, the name 'Saorla' is pronounced *seer-la*.

'The Order' refers to the Orange Order: 'a Protestant fraternity with members throughout the world.'
(www.grandorangelodge.co.uk)

Also, 'calving an iceberg' is not a typographical error. ;)

1: Sleeping Arrangements

Twin or double?" Sean asked.

Keeping her phone to her ear, Saorla Tierney picked up the dishcloth and wiped invisible crumbs from the kitchen worktop. The question was innocent enough, she supposed. "Whichever's cheapest, darlin'."

"They both cost the same."

"Oh, right..." Usually, when she went over for a visit, she stayed with Sean, but those were ordinary visits, not the occasion of her grandson's baptism. "I don't want to leave you out of pocket."

"You're not," Sean assured her. "It's a decent hotel, but it's not expensive. You and Aunty Aileen can stay here, if you'd rather."

"You haven't the space, have you?"

"I've the same space as always, Mummy. I thought you might like some privacy."

A flush of heat shot up Saorla's chest and neck and filled her cheeks. "Twin," she confirmed curtly. She would not have this conversation with her youngest son, never mind that he was forty-three and old enough to know better.

"Are you sure now?"

Not too old to go over her knee, though. "Yes, Sean, I'm quite sure."

"Or you can have my place for the weekend and I'll stay in the hotel. How about that?"

"Don't be daft. I'll be needing to keep an eye on your brother, anyway. So, I'll let you get on. When—"

Sean cut her off. "Hold on. Finn's coming?"

"Didn't he tell you?"

"Did he f—"

"Now then…"

Sean's angry huff made the line crackle. "No, he didn't tell me. When would he?"

"You know, if you spoke to each other from time to time…" Saorla said, pointless as ever it was, which was why she'd left mentioning Finn's intentions until the end of their call.

"I invited him to the baptism, didn't I?" Sean argued.

"Yes, darlin', you did."

"Then the ball's in his court."

"And he's coming."

"So?"

There was no 'so', but Sean's voice had taken on that deep, gruff defensiveness she remembered not so fondly from his—and Finn's—teens. "The two of you can spend some quality time together on neutral ground."

"Neutral? Here? He won't see it that way, will he? I'm not sure I do, to be quite honest."

"So to speak. It's not here, that's what I mean."

"Aye, true enough," Sean relented and was quiet a moment further while he absorbed the news. "Do I need to book a room for him as well?"

"I'd say so. He's bringing Erin along…"

"More like she's bringing him."

She ignored his nit-picking. "They're making a holiday of it. Finn's never been to England, as you know."

"If only he'd had somewhere to stay…" Sean muttered sarcastically. "Are he and Erin back together?"

"Your guess is as good as mine. Maybe you could ask him yourself when you call him about his room requirements." She forged on so Sean couldn't protest. "Right, darlin', I'm going for real this time. I need to get—" she switched out 'Finn's tea on' for "—the washing in before it starts raining. When should I expect those plane tickets?" She'd insisted on paying for them, but Sean was better with online things than she was. Next would be the infernal back and forth with him trying to return the money she'd transferred to his account.

"How's Finn getting here?" he asked.

"He's taking the ferry."

"Oh, right. Well, I made last post yesterday, so they should arrive tomorrow."

"I'll keep an eye out, then. Love to you and Sophie, and my wee man."

"Love you, Mum. Bye now."

"Bye." Saorla checked the call had disconnected and put her phone back in her bag, but the conversation continued to play on her mind as she peeled the potatoes and set them in a pan to boil. Living in England had put some funny ideas in Sean's head, for sure, but he'd never been so brazen before. Or maybe she was making mountains out of molehills. She'd have called Aileen to see what she thought, but Finn was due to arrive anytime now.

He'd left for the clinic first thing, and he should've been back a few hours since. Pub or betting office was where he'd be, until his belly drove him home. That was how it had always been, and would no doubt remain so for the rest of Saorla's days, in spite of Finn having his own place. It was rare for him to spend a night there, but not that surprising; he knew which side his bread was buttered, besides which, thirty years divorced—and before that left to bring up her sons single-handed—Saorla understood the loneliness well enough.

To be fair, Finn was trying, and Sean was being the difficult one for a change. Not that much of a change, now she thought on; since Finn's accident, the two of them had constantly been at loggerheads, and a lot of it was Sean feeling he had to stand up to his big brother whether Finn was in the wrong or not.

She didn't have a favourite. Mothers should love their children equally; she'd always believed that. They thought otherwise, of course, and sometimes it was hard to treat them the same when

Finn needed so much more, on a practical level, at least. Truth be told, they were as bad as each other, and after so long resisting the urge to bang their heads together, she didn't hold out much hope of the two of them ever becoming pals, but if they could make it through the baptism without a set-to, that would be grand.

It was only when the front door opened that Saorla remembered the potatoes, which didn't even have a lid on them, and they were all but boiled dry. "That you, Finn?" she called and grabbed a fork. The click of Finn's crutch preceded his answer.

"No, Mum, it's the bogeyman."

"Well, you look just like Finn Tierney," she responded, as usual. The potatoes were soft enough—a bit crispy on the bottom, but they'd be fine once they were mashed up with the Sunday leftovers from the fridge. She passed Finn on her way to get them. She didn't need to ask how the pain was today; the lips drawn tight over clenched teeth told her all she needed to know.

"Sean's going to phone you about booking the hotel," she said on her way back to the stove.

Leaning his crutch against the table, Finn pulled out a chair, holding his words until he'd eased into it. "He already did."

"Did he now?"

"He did, aye. Couldn't you have told him?"

"I wasn't sure if you'd be needing separate rooms."

"I'm a grown man, Mum."

She had her back to him, but his tone was light, so she ventured further. "Are you an item again?"

"Trial period, so says Erin."

"That's probably wise."

"For her. Not for me. Or you."

"What's it got to do with me?"

"Don't you want me out from under your feet?"

This time, his tone was more cutting, and Saorla's guilt gave her a jolt. "If I wanted you to leave, I'd tell you so." Better he be a living burden than a dead one, and for that thought, she refused to feel guilty after the strain of the past few months. God only knew where they'd have been without Erin and Aileen. When she realised Finn had said no more, she asked, "So you're getting a double room, then?"

"Aye. Right next door to yous, so yous'd best behave yourselves."

"Finn!" She spun to face him, furious and horrified. His grin lingered briefly before he looked away, shame-faced.

"I'm joking with you, Mum."

"Did your brother put you up to it?"

"What?"

"It's funny you both have something to say about it today."

"Sean didn't say a word, and even if he had, would it matter?"

"I don't know what the pair of you think's going on. I'm a seventy-one-year-old woman, for Christ's sake."

"And that means you don't have needs?"

Saorla's face was burning, and so was the tea. She turned back to the stove and flipped the leftovers to brown the other side. "It's not up for discussion—with you or Sean. Do you understand?"

"There's nothing wrong with—"

"I said, do you understand?" She glared over her shoulder.

Finn raised his hands in surrender. "Fine. I won't bring it up again. You have my word."

2: Aileen

I'M SO SORRY, *Aileen. I didn't want to bring trouble to your door."*
Saorla could barely catch a breath in the flood of tears, but
wished her sobbing was loud enough to drown out the banging of
fists and Jim's bellowed insults.

"Come on now, my love. Come away through here." With an
arm around her shoulders, Aileen steered Saorla through to the
kitchen and deposited her at the table. The ignition clicked on the
stove, lighting a ring of blue flame that spat and sparked a protest
against the wet kettle.

The front door rattled in its frame as Jim hammered another
three, four, five times. "Saorla Tierney! I know you're in there! You
want to act like a man, face me like one."

"Oh, God. Please go away," Saorla beseeched, but her voice,
clotted with tears, didn't carry beyond the wad of wet tissue she
clutched in shaking hands. Sure, she'd have faced him 'like a man'
if it were only herself she had to worry about. But it wasn't fair
on the boys, or Aileen. "We'll go to the women's refuge," she said.
"Once he's gone."

"You'll do no such thing!" Aileen admonished sharply.

"But Jim—"

"Is a drunk and a bully, and you've put up with his nonsense
long enough."

"He's right, though, Aileen. I'm no better than him."

"Oh, is that so? Tell me, when was the last time you stayed out
all night? Or had a night out at all?"

Saorla laughed bleakly. "My hen night."

"Right, so, fifteen years ago. Meanwhile, your man's been out
every night, near enough."

"He works hard."

"And you don't?"

"The boys are older now. They look after themselves, more or less..." The tears took over again. "I'm such a bad mother."

Aileen's arms came around her, cradling and rocking. "Hush now. Don't listen to any of them. They don't know what they're saying, and if they're fools enough to take Jim Tierney's word, they're not worth the bother. You're a wonderful mother, Saorla. A wonderful mother. Just ask your Finn and Sean."

"But they need their dad."

"No, my love. They need you. Only you."

"I could stay," Saorla reasoned. "Just until Sean turns sixteen."

"Another six years?"

"It's not so long."

"You'll end up killing the bastard, if he doesn't kill you first."

"It'd be a blessed release. Oh, God, Aileen, what am I to do?"

Aileen's face crumpled. She cupped Saorla's head and pressed it to her breast. "Don't you dare talk like that."

"I'm sorry..."

"And stop being sorry. You've done nothing wrong. Are you listening? Nothing. Stay here with me, it'll all be fine. You'll see..."

***

Saorla stretched an arm out of the bed to silence the alarm's bleep. She'd been awake for hours again; that made it every night since the phone call with Sean, and they were flying to England today. It was silly, getting this worked up. The boys knew—had always known—of her friendship with Aileen, how close they were. How could they not?

She'd taken her godmotherly duties very seriously, had Aileen. All the while Jim was away gambling, drinking, womanising, it had been Aileen at Saorla's side, making tea while Saorla made ends meet, doing the school run, helping with homework, offering a shoulder—so much a part of their family life that it was the boys who had taken it upon themselves to call her 'Aunty'.

There'd have been no question in Sean's mind about inviting Aileen to Dylan's baptism. She was family, simple as that.

Of course, back then, there'd also been no questions and no meaning to them sharing a bed when Aileen stayed over because Jim hadn't come home. The first time he rolled in, in the middle of the night, to discover his side of the bed taken, he'd thought it was one of the boys. Thank God he'd been blind drunk and hadn't noticed Finn and Sean top and tailing on the sofa, where they'd been waiting up so they could give him what for. Thank God, too, that they'd fallen asleep before he'd tumbled through the door.

Saorla circled her wrist in remembrance of the friction burns Jim had gifted her that night—the reason for her sons' derring-do though they were only eight and four years old at the time. It was something else they'd never talked about, their father's brutality. How often had she confessed and begged for God's forgiveness, wishing she could ask it of Finn and Sean but afraid that if she mentioned it, she'd hurt them more than she already had?

Such was the shame she carried for staying until it was too late, but she'd never imagined Jim would raise a hand to his sons. One strike was all he got. He'd gone for Finn, fourteen by then, and Saorla had stepped between them, not the helpless, feeble woman Jim had insisted she was, but a murderess in waiting.

Lay one finger on my children, and I swear, it'll be the last thing you do.

She'd meant it. Every word. She'd have gone to prison if that was what it took to protect Finn and Sean. Were it not for Aileen, sooner or later, that was where she'd have landed.

Jim's story—she'd left him 'for another woman'—was a cover for his bruised ego, nothing more. All those times Aileen had stayed over, he'd seen her, naked even, yet never questioned why. His wife was a frigid old crow, after all, and if she didn't want it from him, why would she take to bedding another, especially a woman?

They were young then; young and beautiful, agile, lithe, passionate...what had happened between them came from the pain they'd shared, the love and trust born of friendship, and need. God, how they'd needed.

When, finally, Saorla found a house for her and the boys, and they'd moved out of Aileen's, there had been no celebration. Just one last night of tears and clinging to each other, more grateful than ever for the time they'd been given now it had come to an end.

The world was a very different place these days, but it was not God's will, although, as Aileen always said, not even St. Paul could bring himself to name the 'unnatural relations' of women. It was easier back then to believe what they were doing wasn't a sin—before the pride parades and the votes for marriage, and before Finn asked the question that branded them with the truth.

No, Saorla was not a lesbian. She could love a man—she *had* loved Jim, God rest his rotten soul, and she'd loved Cian, though he was off his rocker. If she hadn't been so besotted, she'd never have let him move in, because getting the swine to move out again...well, she hadn't. He'd gone of his own accord after Sean went off to university and Finn's behaviour had become intolerable.

The boys didn't know that; Saorla had told them she'd sent Cian packing, more dismayed than guilty that she'd fallen for another eejit who would judge her sons lacking for surviving the only ways they knew how. From there on, she'd sworn off men... other than a few dates with Dermot Sheehan from church, at which point she concluded his wife must've died from boredom.

She still felt sorry for the poor man—who was retired now and drawing a good pension—but that was all she felt: sympathy. And if nothing else, Dermot's loitering had been enough to convince Aileen that Cian was gone for good, though Saorla didn't believe for one minute she'd been forgiven. Seeing as they'd be sharing a room for the next seven days, she'd find out soon enough.

3: Flighty

WELL, ISN'T THIS nice?" Aileen patted Saorla's hand, maintaining contact as she leaned back in her seat and regarded the plane as if it were a grand palace.

"Anyone would think you'd never flown before."

"Listen to you, clocking up the old air miles there."

"Aye, well, it's cheaper these days to fly."

"Cheaper still if you've nowhere to fly to," Aileen pointed out.

"I don't know," Saorla tormented, "Brendan would give you a fine welcome, so he would."

"Jesus. Never again." Aileen was dramatically aghast at the very idea.

Saorla chuckled. "Where's he living now? Still in Wales?"

"No, he moved to Liverpool, didn't he?"

"Did he?"

"To be near their Lottie. I'm sure I told you."

"If you did, I don't recall. In fact, I don't recall you saying Lottie was in Liverpool."

"Are you sure?"

"My memory's not what it was, Aileen."

"Aye, well, she's been there a few years now. Her husband passed his law degree, didn't he? He's working at the courthouse. Brendan's not impressed one bit, as you can imagine."

"I'd have thought it'd come in handy, having a lawyer in the family."

"He's not fully fledged. An usher or something. Clerk, maybe. I don't pay much attention, if I'm honest." Aileen gasped and wagged a finger in the air. "Oh, you've just reminded me. I didn't tell you about Don Reagan, did I?"

Saorla drew breath to answer—yes, she had, if it was the story Saorla was thinking of, although with Aileen's love of gossip, it could be an entirely new saga, not that it mattered, seeing as Aileen had gone on anyway.

"So Don's heart attack just before Christmas, then. You know what caused it, don't you?"

"Pushing his son's car…" Saorla said—both proof she was listening and that she'd heard the story before.

"Right, which he wouldn't have been doing if he was still on the Motability. He's suing the government for negligence. The government!"

"He's not going to win, is he? It'll set a precedent."

"I thought we had a prime minister, not a precedent." Aileen gave Saorla a twinkly eyed grin and chortled at her own joke.

"God, you're a case." Saorla joined in with the laughter. She'd always appreciated Aileen's sense of humour. It had brought her through some tough times—the toughest of all being the months following Finn's accident at nineteen. The doctor's honesty—about Finn's slim chances of survival and, should he make it, ever having anything near a normal life again—was less an acute blow than a constant chafing that left her raw. Even now, she couldn't process how close she'd come to losing a son. Her brain refused to believe it, though she was aware, looking back to that time, that she'd smothered Sean with the love she'd held back from Finn for fear of the unthinkable.

"Are we eating?" Aileen asked.

Saorla emerged from her meanderings to find a stewardess progressing along the aisle with a trolley. "We ate before we left home, and it's only an hour we'll be in the air."

"It's the done thing, when you're on a plane."

Saorla wrinkled her nose. "I'm not hungry, but I might take a drink."

The stewardess edged another row closer; Aileen leaned sideways, her face less than an inch from Saorla's ear, and muttered, "Douglas beach."

Saorla smiled at the shared memory of the Isle of Man holiday they took the year after she left Jim. They were planning a day out, and the boys had wanted to go to the beach.

"Douglas beach is all full of pebbles," Aileen had said and then noticed Sean's worried frown. "But we can still go if you want."

"Was he hungry?"

"Who?"

"Douglas."

"What're you talking about, dafty?"

"He must've been hungry to eat all those pebbles..."

"That was our last holiday together," Saorla mused.

"Aye, it was." Aileen gave a wistful sigh, seemingly studying the back of the seat in front. "I was thinking—"

"Would you like anything to eat or drink?" the stewardess asked, drawing up alongside with a worn but cheery smile.

"Coffee for me, please," Saorla said.

"Same here, please."

"Just ordinary coffee?"

"That's fine," Saorla confirmed for the both of them. It hadn't gone unnoticed that Aileen was a little more subdued than before. She'd something on her mind, for sure.

The stewardess handed over two paper cups with lids, and Saorla paid, pleasantly surprised by how little it cost—relative to what she'd expected. Once the trolley had rolled past, she prompted, "You were saying..."

"Idle thoughts."

Saorla turned as far as her safety belt would allow and studied Aileen's troubled profile. They'd not spent quality time together in a while, or not away from curious ears, so Mass didn't count.

Aileen kept her eyes on the path her finger was tracing around the lid of her cup. "Why didn't we go away together more often?"

"Money?" Saorla suggested. "Or lack of it. And Finn, of course. And your mother."

Aileen's mouth opened and closed in a couple of false starts before she said, "May I ask you something? It's a wee bit delicate."

"Go on," Saorla agreed warily and sipped her coffee for distraction.

"If it had come to worst in January, would you have moved to England?"

Saorla lifted her drink away from her mouth and rubbed her chest to relieve the sudden reflux brought on by Aileen's question. As if it wasn't bad enough to have her son at death's door the once, the fool had to go and do it all over again. In those long, silent hours at the hospital, waiting for Finn to speak, to explain himself or put their minds at ease, the thought had flitted like an alluring, uncatchable butterfly amid the awful mess of their lives: move away, start anew, enjoy her retirement before she was too old.

"I miss Sean and Dylan something terrible," she admitted. "And, I suppose, there'd have been no reason for me to stay in Derry. Well, I say no reason..." Saorla turned again to look Aileen in the eye.

"I hope you wouldn't have stayed for my sake," Aileen teased lightly.

Saorla smiled. "Don't do yourself down."

"I'm not, my love. Your sons are more important than anyone or anything else—as it should be."

"I doubt any of us would've made it this far without you." Saorla sought Aileen's hand and gave it a light but sure squeeze. Aileen curled her fingers around Saorla's, keeping hold as the plane began its descent, to the accompaniment of the pilot's announcement that they'd be landing at Liverpool John Lennon Airport in ten minutes.

"So, I've a question for you now," Saorla said.

"What's that, then?"

"Well, it's buried under a big mound of ifs, but...if I'd gone, and if you didn't have your mum, would you have come with me?"

"Oh...there *is* a question." Aileen freed herself from Saorla's grasp and swapped her coffee to the other hand. With a grimace, she flexed her fingers and peered out of the window. "See, I could've told you it was raining without looking."

"You looked anyway."

"True enough. I wonder what Brendan's up to this week?"

Saorla pursed her lips. She'd got the gist, or, at least, Aileen had confirmed her question-dodging had nothing to do with not wanting to be within spitting distance of her long-ago ex-fiancé. When she'd broken off the engagement, she'd told Brendan she was joining a convent. Of course, she never did; nor had she been with another man since. It was an unintentional cruelty, for while Brendan had married and remarried, and had children and grandchildren, his heart still belonged to Aileen, whereas Aileen's belonged...well, perhaps it was best not dwelt upon.

4: Blighty

ALWAYS LOOKING FOR a way to save a penny or two—or a bit more on this occasion—Saorla had told Sean to stay at home until she called him to confirm they'd landed. Paying to park and wait at the airport was pointless expense when they couldn't be sure they'd arrive on time, although they had only their hand luggage—they'd sent their outfits in the post a couple of weeks in advance—so went straight through Arrivals.

Phone in hand, Saorla hooked arms with Aileen and steered her out of the flow of foot traffic to make the call.

"Ahem!" Aileen pointed across to the exit doors, where Sean was standing and looking in entirely the wrong direction.

Saorla sighed, exasperated. "Why will he never do as he's damn well told?"

"Takes after his mother, so he does," Aileen chanced and scurried after Saorla, who was marching with purpose towards her youngest son.

"Oy, you! What're you doing here?" she asked sharply. He grinned and moved in to give her a hug and a kiss. "Your charms won't work on me, Sean Tierney," she claimed in words muffled by his shoulder, her crossness already diminished.

"You all right, Mum?"

"I suppose," she said, still doing her best to sound stern.

Sean released her to hug Aileen and then took both of their bags. "How are you doing, Aunty Aileen? It's lovely to see you."

"And you, Sean. And I'm grand, thanks for asking. Yourself?"

"I'm smashing, thanks. All right, so, we're this way." He gestured and moved off, glancing back to check they were following. Early Saturday evening, the airport was busy, and they walked almost the full length of the car park before they reached Sean's car.

"Isn't this flash?" Aileen ran her hand along the roof.

"It's a decent runner," Sean said. "Pretty basic, though."

"You gave it a wash just for us, did you?"

Sean's smile was his answer, and soon after, they discovered he'd gone the whole hog and got it valeted, too. Saorla, in the front seat, gave Sean a sideways once-over.

He briefly made eye contact before switching his attention to his seat belt. "What's up?"

"Cat can look at a king," she retorted and dealt with her own seat belt.

"Are you fit in the back?" Sean called over his shoulder.

"I am," Aileen confirmed. Saorla couldn't turn enough to see her, but she sounded happy as a pig in muck.

Sean started the engine and reversed out of the space; Saorla kept watch in her peripheral vision. He had something to say and was waiting for a good moment to say it.

"Have you eaten?" he asked once they were on the motorway.

"Not since home."

"Right. We were thinking, we'll get you checked in, and have tea at the pub. They do a great two meals for one on steak."

Aileen gave a needy groan. "I haven't had a steak in ages."

Saorla bit her tongue. She'd almost said 'me neither', which was the truth. The household budget didn't run to more than the essentials, and that was with all the extra bits and bobs Sean kept sneaking into her account. On the one hand, she wished he wouldn't; he was her son, after all, and it was topsy-turvy. On the other, she was grateful; she'd have lost the house by now. Her pension and Finn's meagre contribution—if he could make one at all—was barely enough to cover the bills.

"Who's 'we'?" she asked.

Sean pulled out and around a slow lorry, and listed aloud, "Soph, Dylan, Hay—"

"That's the godmother?" Aileen asked.

"Aye. She and Soph went to school together."

"Do you know her, Saorla?"

"I haven't had the pleasure, I don't think."

"No, you haven't," Sean confirmed. "One of a kind, she is. She's staying in the hotel as well, but nowhere near you, you'll be pleased to know."

"Don't you start that again," Saorla warned.

Sean made a quick manoeuvre back into the inside lane; a sports car zoomed by at an unnecessary speed. "Start what, Mummy?" he asked, innocent as anything.

"You know what."

For his part, Sean looked puzzled, but then something clicked. "Oh! No, that's not what I meant at all. I was talking about Hay's nine-year-old triplets."

"Jesus, Mary and Joseph…"

"Ash, Kai and Sage, actually," Sean said with a grin.

"Funny," Saorla muttered dryly, though she was amused, as was Aileen, who fairly had the giggles.

"So, anyway," Sean continued, "Hay'll be there with her three. Then there's Josh, George and Libby."

"It better be a big pub," Aileen said.

"It's a decent size, but it won't be a problem. It's our local, and they know us."

"I bet they do."

Sean's gaze lingered on the rear-view mirror. "You know I'm teetotal now, don't you, Aunty Aileen?"

"Are you?" she asked, even though she did know. Saorla was very proud of Sean for kicking the booze, and it wasn't something to be freely shared with anyone, although she'd told Aileen enough times for her to come back with a sarcastic, 'Has he? No!' whenever Saorla mentioned it.

"Coming up on three years," Sean said.

"Very good." A couple of minutes passed by with only the noise of the road, and then Aileen asked, "So, how far are we now?"

Saorla chuckled. "Oh, God, what's she like?"

"I don't know where I am, do I?"

"Even so, you're a bit long in the tooth to be asking 'Are we there yet?'"

"About another twenty minutes," Sean said.

"Oh, well, that's not so far at all."

Sean glanced in the mirror again and then at Saorla, his smile fond, and sweet as it had always been. In her mind, he'd never aged a day, though his hair was taking on the same dusty appearance as his brother's—a prelude to the lovely dark silver their grandad's had turned, and which Saorla's was, too, under the black dye. Sometimes keeping on top of those shiny roots was more trouble than it was worth, but she wasn't ready to go grey.

"I take it your brother's not arrived yet?"

"He called a couple of hours ago to say they'd just got off the ferry and were stopping somewhere for food." Sean flicked the indicator for the next turnoff. "I did tell him we were hoping to head out this evening, but he said Erin couldn't wait."

"That's a shame." Saorla was surprised how matter-of-fact she sounded when she was absolutely overjoyed that her boys were communicating like adults. Of course, it should've been a given at their age, but the damage from Finn's accident extended far beyond his shattered legs and the tremendous weight of guilt he'd lugged around for the past twenty-nine years.

It wasn't right, she knew, but she was more tolerant of Finn's hostility towards his brother than of it coming back at him. It was easier to forgive when he'd lost so much, and, truth be told, she placed too-high expectations on Sean, as if his being a psychologist by trade meant he should have a better handle on such matters in his own life. The poor lad had gone from trouble-free teenager to man of the house almost overnight. He'd left school and gone out to work, denied those few years when he was old enough to be independent and still young enough to enjoy it, but he'd kept on smiling.

That was the way Sean had always been, doing what was necessary without complaint—up to the point he'd lost his big brother, because the Finn who left the hospital was not the same one who'd left the house for a night out with his mates. Sean had grieved and then erected a wall between them. Saorla knew, because she'd done the same with their dad the first time he turned on her to deflect from his own misdemeanours. The maternal bond was like X-ray specs, seeing past the lies, the sniping and bravado, to the hiding, frightened little boys beneath, whose fights were about so much more than protecting their mum or feeling hard done by, and she prayed daily they'd find a way to resolve their differences, even if she didn't live to see it.

"That's where I live, Aunty Aileen. Third from the end."

"Oh, right."

Saorla watched the terrace flash by, to be replaced by fields, the wee church, the primary school, more fields...

"And coming up on the left is the pub."

"The Red Lion. Very English."

"That it is," Sean agreed. "This is the village, then." He barely reaching the end of the sentence before they'd passed through it. "The hotel's a couple of miles on, so you could walk it to ours if you're feeling spritely."

"A couple of miles? Pfft. That's nothing. I walk that twice a day to see my mum."

"She does," Saorla concurred, like Sean would doubt Aileen's word.

"No wonder you're so fit, Aunty Aileen. That's a trek to be doing every day."

"You do what you have to."

"True enough."

Which isn't always what you want, Saorla thought, although truthfully, before Aileen's question on the flight, moving closer to Sean and Dylan had been no more than a fleeting thought. It was a nice area, for sure—not too posh, though the people were better off than back home. And there was a big town nearby, with decent public transport. She could live there quite happily...in the right circumstances. But whichever way she looked at it, the costs were too great.

5: Piety

SEAN TURNED OFF the road and through a gateway framed by tall, intricately fretted wrought iron gates, beyond those a driveway leading to a vast, white mansion. As they neared it, Saorla spotted a sign pointing to the 'hotel reception'.

"We are not staying here."

"You are," Sean answered, as if her statement had been a request for clarification. "Nice, isn't it?"

"We're not staying here, Sean."

"Why? What's wrong with the place?"

"If I'd known you meant here—"

"Where did you think I meant?"

"I don't know. But it costs a bomb, I bet."

"It's really not that expensive, Mummy. Besides, they gave me a group booking discount."

"I don't believe you."

"I swear." He stopped the car. "And anyway, what's the point in me earning all that money if I can't treat you and Aunty Aileen to a bit of a holiday?"

"Darlin'..."

"No, Mum." He was out of the door before she could protest further.

She stewed, listening to the boot swing open then slam shut. Sean stalked past the car and away with their bags.

"What're we doing?" Aileen asked. "Are we getting out?"

Saorla snuffed hard out of her nose. "God only knows." She wasn't going to win this one, but she could still make her disgruntlement clear.

Sean reached the hotel's front entrance and looked back, eyes stormy under a heavy brow. *He looks just like his*—No. She refused to insult him with that thought. His heart was in the right place, however infuriating that was.

Aileen's hand came to a rest on Saorla's shoulder. "Forgive me if I'm out of line, but you're not being very gracious."

Saorla's temper grew a little hotter but was quickly damped by her friend's wise words. She sighed and reached up, laying her hand on top of Aileen's. "I know." She watched Sean marching back to the car. "It's just so damned frustrating. I wouldn't mind if it was the first time he'd ever pulled this trick."

"Remember when he used to bring you mint balls?"

"Oh, God, yes." Saorla laughed at the memory. Every Saturday, he'd gone off to the sweet shop with his pocket money and come back with two ounces of mint balls for his mum. "I hate the things."

"But you never let on, did you?"

The passenger door opened. "Shall I just ask them if they'll serve breakfast in the car park?" Sean asked, attempting to cover his hurt with a wink and a smile.

She flicked her hand at him so he'd give her some space, grabbing his arm to keep her balance as she came into contact with the chunky gravel underfoot. "I'm sorry, darlin'. It was a surprise, that's all."

"A lovely one," Aileen added. She, too, got out, and carefully pushed the door shut, polishing away any fingerprints with her sleeve.

"Aye, a lovely one," Saorla agreed, shaking her head at Aileen's oddity as the three of them stepped off together. "Won't you be needing your keys?" They were still hanging from the ignition.

"Why?"

"What if someone helps themselves?"

"They won't."

Saorla couldn't believe he was prepared to chance it; nevertheless, she followed him inside to the reception desk.

"Good evening, Mr. Tierney."

"A good evening to you." He beamed his most charming smile at the young woman behind the desk, who blushed and scuffled together a pile of papers.

"Welcome, Mrs. Tierney and Miss Cullen. If you could check the information on these forms and sign and date at the bottom, please."

"Sure." Fishing her glasses from her handbag, Saorla took the pen and forms, and scanned through the details Sean must've given to the hotel, signing where indicated. She handed both pen and glasses to Aileen.

"Ah, you know me too well, my love." Aileen put on the glasses but still had to lean away from the page to see. "I'm not even sure I packed mine." She signed without reading and pushed the forms back to the receptionist.

"Thank you, ladies. Breakfast is between seven and ten, and we also serve lunch and dinner—you'll find all of the information in the booklet in your room, along with the number for room service. Here's your key—room fourteen." The receptionist leaned forward and pointed along a corridor to their left. "Take the lift or stairs to the first floor, turn right and follow the signs."

"Thanks very much," Saorla said, and Aileen parroted. Sean slowly moved off. "You can wait here if you like, darlin'."

"I'll take up your bags."

Again, Saorla bit her tongue, shrewd enough to recognise her own obstinacy when its likeness was reflected back at her, and followed Sean to the lift, which was small and not especially sturdy but sufficed for the three of them.

Whilst the hotel was grand-looking, with flock wallpaper split by glossy dado rails, and plush carpets into which their feet sank, it wasn't huge. Room fourteen was one right turn from the lift, or left turn, depending on whether you were coming or going, and it was just an ordinary room of moderate size, with twin beds made up in white linen, a red cushion atop each. They stayed long enough to deposit their bags, inspect the en suite bathroom and their baptism outfits—already hanging in the wardrobe—and locate the kettle, cups, teabags and wee pots of UHT milk, before they were back out to the car and heading for The Red Lion.

"It's a lovely evening," Aileen observed, and it was. The rain that had accompanied their landing had soon dried up, and the fields on either side of the road glowed gold-green in the sun slowly descending the cloudless sky. "I hope it holds for tomorrow."

"As do I." Saorla folded her arms and stared out the side window at the beige blur of fence posts. She wasn't at all happy that the baptism was being held outside, but she'd complained enough already.

"The forecast says it will," Sean said. "I didn't tell you, did I, Mummy? We've had a slight change of plan."

"Oh? What's that? We're off to some freshwater spring or somewhere else ungodly?"

"Surely a freshwater spring is more godly than a basin carved out of a hunk of marble?"

"In God's house."

"Are not springs part of His creation?"

In the back, Aileen gave an amused but nervous 'ooh-hoo!' Saorla flapped a hand in her general direction to shut her up. It had the opposite effect, provoking a minor giggling fit. "You've got one on you this evening, haven't you?" she snipped at Sean.

"Well, if you'd let me finish…"

"I didn't stop you."

"Fonts are just another example of health and safety gone mad."

"Says who?"

"The Church," Sean argued, adding, "I imagine," as a muttered afterthought.

"So you don't know for sure."

"It's all academic, anyway."

"Everything is to you." They arrived at the pub, and Saorla waited until Sean had parked up before she prompted, "Well?"

He made a big thing of pulling on the handbrake, wobbling the gearstick to check it was in neutral, turning off the ignition, unfastening his seat belt...

"*Sean!*"

"All right, now. There's no need to get in a tizzy. It's a good thing. You'll like it."

"Maybe—if you'd damn well tell me."

"Dylan's being baptised in the chapel."

"Chapel?"

"Aye. It's a lovely—"

"Not a church?"

"It's a small church."

"Catholic?"

"Interdenominational."

"It has a font, though?"

"Font, altar, sanctuary, pews..."

"It'll do, I suppose." Saorla unclipped her seat belt and cast it aside, still peeved, though she had little reason to be. Behind her, Aileen's silence was her judge. *Ungracious.* Quite why she was being so, she didn't know, and the apology was lodged somewhere deep in her throat. Before she said anything else she might regret, she got out of the car and put some distance between it and herself, keeping her back to the conversation that would now be taking place as Sean tried to glean what he'd done to upset her from Aileen. In truth, he'd done nothing; him and his brother in the same place for any length of time always put her on edge.

As she studied the pub before her, trying to get her thoughts in order, a familiar blonde head popped up over the fence to the side of the building.

"Mrs. Tierney!" A hand waggled frantically.

She tutted but finally cracked a smile. "How many times, Joshy? It's *Saorla*!"

"We're in the beer garden. Hold on."

He disappeared from view, reappearing half a minute later at the pub's front door. He came to her—she hadn't moved a muscle—all smiles, arms open. "Hey. It's wonderful to see you."

"You, too." She accepted his hug and cheek kiss. "You're looking well."

Josh released her and stepped back. "As are you. How do you do it? You haven't aged a day!"

Saorla waved dismissively whilst secretly revelling in the compliment. It was a big fib, even if she was 'young for her years'—all the women in her family fared well in that regard—but she'd not even turned fifty when she and Josh had first met.

"What's he doing?" Josh nodded towards the car and Sean, who was still sitting behind the wheel and watching.

"Smarting is what he's doing. If we go in, they'll follow." She gestured to Josh. "Lead the way, young man."

"Young?" Josh repeated as he stepped off, keeping a modest pace.

"What are you now? Thirty-eight?"

"Just turned forty in February."

"You never did!"

"I did." He paused at the door and chewed his cheek in thought. "I don't feel any older. Do I look it?"

"You still look the same to me. Our Sean's little mate from uni."

Josh smiled bashfully and turned rosy pink. "I'm a dad now. Did he tell you?"

"Aye, he told me. Congratulations. I've been looking forward to meeting her."

"Then I won't keep you any longer."

6: While the Sun Shines

THE PUB'S BEER garden was vast, two-thirds of it filled with picnic tables, the other third a children's play area. Saorla's *granny sense* homed in on Dylan, presently descending the slide. He hadn't noticed her arrive, but the girl with him did, and glanced over briefly. Libby.

Saorla recognised her immediately; she was so like Josh it was uncanny—given they weren't blood-related. She was darker in complexion, her chestnut-brown hair a good few shades away from Josh's sandy blonde, and her features were more rounded. Yet simply looking at her triggered Saorla's memory of her first visit to England, not long after Sean had moved there to study.

Whilst Josh was three years Sean's junior—back then only seventeen years old—she'd returned home confident that there were people looking out for her baby. Sure, the friendship had had its ups and downs, as all friendships do, but here they still were.

Sean had always been particular; he was popular and got on well with everyone, but he had no patience for mind games or back-stabbing, and when he committed to a friendship, he gave it his all. Josh was exactly what Sean needed: straight-talking, intuitive and generous to a fault, and whatever differences they'd had, they'd found ways to resolve them. No surprise, then, that Sean had asked Josh to be Dylan's godfather. Much as Saorla would've like nothing more than for Sean to ask his brother, she knew in her heart, even without the love lost between them, Finn wasn't up to the task.

Aileen bumped up behind Saorla. "What've you stopped for?"

"Oh, so you decided to join us, then?"

"We were waiting for you to calm your knickers."

Saorla didn't deign that with a response.

"Want a drink?" Sean asked them both.

"Please, darlin'. A beer for me—it's a warm evening."

"Pint or a glass?"

"A pint? Good God! A glass will do nicely, thank you." Saorla laughed, not quite believing he'd asked her.

"May I have a wine and soda, please, Sean?" Aileen said.

"You may. Won't be long. Go on over, why don't you?" He went inside to order their drinks, leaving them to their own devices, which was when Josh noticed Saorla hadn't followed him to the picnic table where the others were sitting. Josh came back and collected them, and then properly introduced everyone.

"You know Sophie, of course..."

Sophie rose to hug and kiss both women.

"Hmm, I'm not sure," Aileen teased. "Who are ye again?"

Saorla wanted to stamp on Aileen's toes. She could be an insensitive clod at times. As far as Saorla was aware, everything was well between Sean and Sophie, but Aileen had a bee in her bonnet, always asking 'why's that, do you think?' whenever Sophie didn't accompany Sean on his visits home. Aileen had so many bees in her bonnet—mostly about things that didn't concern her—she could've made a packet selling honey.

"And this is George, my husband," Josh introduced.

"I believe we've met," Saorla said with a smile. It was only the once, on her last visit almost two years ago, but she'd been very taken with him. She wasn't the only one.

"We haven't," Aileen said, pushing Saorla aside to reach George and initiating a hug.

He laughed. "We have now."

"And you're married to Josh?"

"Yep."

"Properly married? Like, you know...a *gay* marriage?"

"Um…"

"Aileen!" Saorla hissed. "Sorry, George. Don't mind her. She doesn't mean anything by it."

"OK." George looked a bit fazed. "Here," he said, offering his seat.

"Where will you sit?" Aileen asked.

"I'll pull over another table." He was already on the move. Aileen accepted his invitation; seeing as there was room for the both of them, Saorla did, too.

"I'm Hay," the mystery woman introduced herself before Josh got that far. She remained seated, no hugs or kisses. To be fair, the poor thing looked done in.

"Lovely to meet you. They your three, are they?" Saorla nodded at the trio of trouble scrapping over whose turn it was to have a go on the rope swing.

"Yes," Hay confirmed wearily, pausing to light a roll-up cigarette. "We were on the road for six hours, and they're hungry."

"Ah. Well, they're not doing so bad, then." Saorla winced as one of the triplets pushed another off the swing. There'd be tears before bedtime. Meanwhile, Libby was guiding Dylan down the slide again, subtly watching and listening to the adults. Saorla leaned across to Josh and asked quietly, "Is she all right?"

"A little overwhelmed, but she's fine." Regardless of his assertion, Josh's attention remained on Libby. He might not have looked or sounded much different from his younger self, but he'd certainly softened with age and parenthood.

Sean hadn't told Saorla much about Libby other than she'd run away from her deeply religious parents and had been living on the streets when Josh and George took her in. Whether it was all the people bothering Libby, or the fact they were gathered for a religious occasion, Saorla was undecided—and saddened; her own faith brought her much comfort.

She'd grown up in a large Catholic family, and they were devout. Mass every Sunday even if they were on their death bed;

confession; praying the rosary every night. They read from the Bible, lived by the Commandments and followed Jesus' example. They'd all been baptised and confirmed, and in the entire family, Saorla and Sean were the only divorcees—or the only ones she knew of. She'd had no contact with her siblings or their children since her dad's funeral.

For all of that, she'd tried not to nag Sean about getting Dylan baptised, particularly as Sean didn't bother with church himself, and he'd made it clear he and Sophie had no intention of marrying. With Dylan only two months shy of turning two, to Saorla's mind, they'd left it far too long, never mind that it would be in an interdenominational chapel and the godparents weren't Catholics. They were doing it, and she should be happy about that, or put on a good show, at least.

"Here we are." A glass of ale appeared before her.

"Thank you, darlin'."

"No problem." Sean passed Aileen's drink to her and set down a pile of menus. "Finn's just called. They're an hour away."

"Oh. Good." Saorla ignored the minor chest palpitations brought on by the news. Maybe they'd be all right. It was only for a few days, after all. "Are we to wait for them or eat now?"

"Eat now, I'd say. They can always order when they get here."

"Seems reasonable." She dug her glasses out of her bag, put them on before Aileen snatched them away, and picked up a menu. "Right, what've got here…"

7: Trebles

WOULD YOU LOOK how thick it is! I'll never get through this." Saorla sawed a bite-sized piece off the inch-thick pink-red steak.

"Like calving an iceberg," Josh said.

Saorla laughed. "Aye, you're not wrong there."

In spite of her grumbling, her meal was already half gone, although she'd been sharing her chips with Dylan. He was a good little eater at home—and at his granny's—but he was less than impressed with his kid's meal of fish fingers, potato smileys and peas. Not even the triplets telling him the peas were tiny green eyeballs could persuade him to try them.

"Come on, Dylan. Eat up," Sophie encouraged, which only made him squeeze his eyes tight shut and vigorously shake his head. Sophie sighed and set the spoonful of peas back on the plate. As soon as he heard it touch down, Dylan opened his eyes and grabbed another chip from Saorla's plate. Sophie sighed again. "No table manners, that child."

"Can't imagine where he gets that from," Aileen teased with a wink at Sean, who froze, fork loaded and mouth open in overplayed taking of offence. The steak promptly dropped from the prongs and tumbled all the way down his shirt.

"Ah, Jesus." Swapping fork for napkins, he rubbed at the speckled creamy beige peppercorn sauce trail.

"So who's who, then?" Aileen asked the triplets. "And no telling me fibs now."

"I'm Sage," the one with the darkest hair said. "That's Ash," she gestured to the sibling on the right.

"Are you sure?" Hay asked.

"Yes!" Sage scowled. "And that's Kai."

"Only Sage can tell them apart," Hay explained.

"They are very alike," Aileen observed.

Saorla nearly choked on her laughter…and her steak. "They're identical, Aileen."

"But Sage looks nothing like the other two."

"I'm a singleton," Sage declared proudly.

"You're a what now?"

From the weight of Sage's sigh, it wasn't the first time it had needed explaining. "Mum got IVF with two eggs. I came from one. Ash and Kai came from the other."

"Well I never!" Aileen gazed in astonishment at the identical siblings. "So yous are twin brothers?"

They both shrugged at the same time and continued shovelling down their dinners.

"Sisters?"

They shrugged again. Aileen looked to Saorla in confusion and then startled at Hay's boom of laughter.

"Stick with siblings, and you won't go far wrong," she advised.

"I'm a girl," Sage stated.

"I know you are, sweetheart." Hay smiled fondly and brushed a finger over her daughter's cheek, followed by a sharp, "Kai, stop it!"

"It wasn't me!" the child claimed, but Saorla had seen the trajectory of the airborne pea that skimmed Sage's shoulder before landing on a nearby table. Luckily, the table wasn't in use.

"Have you had enough?" Hay asked. The twin-triplets nodded. "Then you can go and play."

"Please can we have ice cream?" one asked on behalf of them both.

"Just this once, but you'll have to wait till we're all finished."

"'Kay."

"'Kay."

The two of them bolted, straight back to the rope swing.

"Sorry about that." Hay smiled glibly and picked up her fork again. She'd been so busy with her children she'd made little progress with her own meal. Saorla remembered that experience all too well.

"I have to say," Hay waved her fork around the table, "it's glorious to be with so many *family*..." She glanced down at the scant remains on their plates and shuddered. "Even if you are murderers."

"Technically, I'm not family," Aileen corrected.

"I hope you're not a murderer, either, Aunty Aileen," Sean said jovially. Next to him, Sophie was all a-fluster; Saorla couldn't figure out why. Hay had already explained when the rest of them were ordering their steaks that she and the kids were vegan, and her murderers remark was made light-heartedly. Or so Saorla had thought, but clearly she was missing something, because Libby, who was sitting next to Sophie, was staring hard at Josh— to Aileen's left—and George was fussing with clearing away the triplets' dinner plates.

A familiar *click...click...*

As if the atmosphere wasn't tense enough already.

"Looks like we're missing a party here, Erin." Finn stopped behind Sean and peered over his shoulder. "You could've left some for me, you greedy so-and-so."

"Alright, Finn? Good journey?"

"Aye. Not bad."

Sean got up so his brother could sit down, but Finn waved the offer away.

"You carry on. Anyone need a drink?"

Saorla held her breath, waiting for Sean's sarcastic retort.

"I'll get them in," he said. "It's easier."

"Holy Mary..." Saorla muttered and quickly covered her mouth with her napkin. Stuffing it in might've been a wiser move.

"I'll come with you," Erin said, and she and Sean left.

"Out!" Dylan shouted, pulling against the belt keeping him in his high chair.

"Hold on while Mummy goes for a wee," Sophie said.

"I'll deal with him," Saorla offered, already on her feet. She'd been desperate to give him a cuddle all evening.

"If you don't mind."

"Mind?" Saorla laughed.

Sophie sped away to the toilets, calling back, "There's a bottle in the bag if you think he wants it."

"OK," Saorla acknowledged and advanced on her grandson. "Come on, then, little man."

He stretched his arms into the air, and Saorla's heart soared. She unclipped the belt and lifted him free. He immediately snuggled against her shoulder.

"Gosh, you've got big!" she said, trying to hide her tearfulness and ignore the big mushy grin on Aileen's face. She returned to her seat and settled Dylan on her lap.

Finn looked around the table. "Is that free?" He indicated the space next to Libby, previously occupied by the two triplets who weren't Sage—to her shame, Saorla had forgotten their names again.

"I think so," Libby answered, looking to Hay for confirmation.

"Yeah. They won't be back now until they smell ice cream."

Finn hobbled to the end of the bench, laid his crutch on the ground and eased down onto the seat. He held out his hand to Libby. "Good to meet you. I'm Finn."

"I'm Libby. You're Sean's brother."

"So I am."

"He's talked about you."

"I bet he has. All good things, right?" Finn winked playfully.

Libby smiled. "Right. You sound exactly the same."

"Aside from his waffle and all his big fancy words."

"And you talk way faster."

"Should I slow it down a wee bit?"

After a few seconds' pause, Libby answered, "No, it's OK."

Saorla's scalp felt tight from her hitched eyebrows. It was only the second time Libby had spoken since they'd arrived, the first being to tell George what she wanted to eat. As for Finn—maybe he'd missed his calling. Saorla had never seen him so sociable, certainly not around young people, although usually there were none around for him to be sociable with.

It might've been different if she'd stayed with Jim. They'd wanted more babies, but it wasn't to be, and not for want of trying—at first. Then there were the cousins whom Finn and Sean hadn't seen since they were children themselves; some they hadn't met at all. It was a shame things had gone that way, but there was nothing to be done about it. Had Jim left her rather than the other way around, it would still have been her fault for not doing more to keep him.

How glad she was that times had changed and the Church no longer expected women to stay in loveless marriages, even if it was taking a while for everyone else to catch on.

"So who are all these people, young Libby?" Finn asked.

"This is Hay—Dylan's...godmum?"

"Spiritual guardian," Hay corrected.

"And this is George..."

While Libby continued with the introductions, Aileen folded her arms and surreptitiously prodded Saorla in the side, nodding meaningfully in Finn's direction. No doubt they were both thinking the same thing: it couldn't last.

8: Troubles

FINN SMILED HELLOS at everyone, lingering long on Hay's ample, bra-less breasts, before returning his gaze to Josh. "So you're the nephew's godfather, then."

"Yes."

"I hope you're up to the task."

"Sean seems to think so."

"Us Tierney men can be quite a handful, eh, Mum?"

Saorla jigged Dylan on her knees, keeping her eyes on him, not Finn. "I'm sure Josh is well aware of the commitment he's making."

Finn raised his hands peaceably. "Aye, no doubt. You've known our Sean a good while, haven't you?"

"Twenty-three years."

"From uni?"

"That's right."

"Thought so. Your name crops up quite often."

Sean and Erin returned with the drinks and distributed them, their prior smiles and chatter swiftly strangled by the tension around the table.

"This mine?" Finn asked and picked up the pint in front of him. At Erin's nodded confirmation, he took a long swig and sighed in deep satisfaction. "You believe in all this God nonsense, do you, Josh?"

"Erin was telling me the trip over was a bit rough," Sean said.

Finn smirked. "That's a no, then."

"Do you believe in God, Finn?" Libby asked. Sean sagged into his seat, while Josh looked proud as Punch.

43

"You're asking in front of me ma?" Finn sent a grin Saorla's way.

She narrowed her eyes, no idea if he was tormenting. She'd understand if he didn't believe—his accident had tested even her faith—but she still held out hope for both of her sons' souls.

Finn shrugged. "I suppose I do. I mean, all that science stuff you believe in—" he nodded at Sean "—is an act of faith. Gravity, the Big Bang, the mysteries of the human brain..." His tone had taken on a mystical quality. "Science doesn't do any better coming up with explanations."

"It goes about it a different way," Sean argued.

"Aye, true enough. But it's nice to think the big man's up there looking out for us." Finn paused to peer at the sky and then took another drink. "Mind you, you've got to wonder what kind of cruel bastard He is."

"Finn! Language!"

"Sorry, Mum...ladies."

"I've heard worse," Libby said with a hint of mischief. "When Josh and Sean are arguing, they swear loads."

"Is that right?" Finn shook his head. "Yous ought to be ashamed of yourselves."

"Let he who is without sin..." Sean began.

"You're a fine one to talk!" Finn raised his glass at his brother.

"Aye, thanks for the reminder."

"I was toasting. Here's to your health." Finn did it again. Saorla felt a headache coming on.

Aileen wagged her finger at the two of them. "Boys, that's enough."

"We're just having a bit of fun," Finn protested.

Sean eyed his brother for a moment and then picked up his own glass, which contained lemonade, or lime and soda maybe. He lifted it. "Up yours," he said.

Finn clanged his pint against Sean's, and they both glugged heartily.

The banter continued. It was too close to the bone for Saorla's liking—and a few others besides, not least Josh, who kept his mouth firmly shut until the landlord rang the bell for last orders. Even then, he opened it just long enough to wish everyone a goodnight and then he, George and Libby were away.

"Are you ready, Finn?" Erin asked. She'd been chatting with Hay and Sophie, interspersed with cutting glares at Finn whenever she caught him staring at Hay's breasts. If Saorla was honest, she was having a problem ignoring them herself. In the cool of the late evening, Hay's t-shirt left little to the imagination.

"Well?" Erin pushed Finn for an answer.

"Whenever Mum and Aunty Aileen are."

"We're waiting on you."

"In that case…" Finn downed the rest of his pint and leaned heavily on the table to heave to his feet. "We'll be seeing ye in the morrow, then," he said to Sean.

"Aye, bright and early."

Sophie collected Dylan—asleep in Saorla's arms—and put him in his pushchair. He didn't stir. With a hug for Hay, she said, "I'll see you back home, Sean."

"All right. Won't be long."

"Why, where are you off?" Aileen asked.

"Taking Hay and her three back to the hotel."

"Oh, silly me."

"You behave yourself now." Finn gave Sean an elbow nudge and tilted his head in Hay's direction. Hay's roar of laughter filled the empty beer garden.

"Don't worry about me, Finn. I'm in safe hands with your brother."

Finn's gaze dropped to Hay's breasts again. Erin gripped him by his earlobe. He inhaled sharply and closed one eye, which made Hay laugh all the more. She stepped towards him, leaned close to his unencumbered ear and said very slowly, "I'm a lesbian."

***

45

What a joy to finally get into bed. With a cup of tea apiece and a wee packet of biscuits between them, they relaxed in companionable near-silence. Through the open window, they heard the occasional car pass by, the hoot of an owl.

Aileen tugged the cord dangling next to her pillow, turning the light off and then on again. "I might get one of these at home."

Off, on.

Off, on.

"Aileen!"

She chuckled. "Sorry, my love. You know what they say about small things."

Saorla settled back against her pillow and let her eyes close.

"Don't you be asleep with that cup in your hand."

"Me? Waste a cup of tea? Do I even know you?"

"It's been a long day," Aileen reasoned.

"It has," Saorla agreed, but she wasn't at all sleepy, replaying the evening in her mind. Sometimes she felt too old for the world, as if time was moving on without her—Sean and Sophie having a child out of wedlock, Josh and George being allowed to marry and adopt Libby, Hay's man-free conception and just coming right out and saying it.

Not that Saorla was judging. To each their own: that was her philosophy. Yet, in God's eyes—and hers—a marriage was a sacred union within which the miracle of life could happen. One man, one woman. She wasn't dismissing Josh and George's love, nor casting aspersions on Hay's choice to go it alone, and she'd have been grand with Sean and Sophie's decision were he not her own son. But in the end, it was none of her business.

Of course, she'd have liked a wedding.

"Are you waiting for me, Aileen?"

"Oh, no. You just take your time. I can fall asleep with the light on."

"You could fall asleep in the middle of the road, but that's not what I meant."

"What did you mean?"

"Are you waiting for me to make some kind of big decision?"

"What are you talking about?"

"You know. About us being...more like Josh and George."

"What, married? God, no!" Aileen's horror was both reassuring and disappointing. "I mean, sure, it'd be nice to spend more time together, maybe even share a place, but I don't want to think about what awful things need to happen to make that possible." Aileen shuffled down her bed and adjusted her pillows. "I know what's troubling you."

"You do?"

"Always, my love. She used that word, didn't she?"

"Who and what word?" Saorla bluffed.

"The L-word."

"There's nothing wrong with two women showing each other affection."

"His Holiness says not."

"It's the flaunting I don't like." Saorla drained her cup and set it on the bedside table.

"Nobody was flaunting." Aileen reached up to switch off the light as if it would stop Saorla arguing back. She had no intention of doing so and instead lay down and rolled onto her side.

"Don't you be sleeping on your back now."

Her warning prompted a chuckle, followed by movement. Aileen had taken heed, which was as well. She snored something terrible.

"Saorla?"

"Hmm?"

Passing traffic, that wee owl out there somewhere, the creaking of pipes, a door closing along the corridor...

"Nothing."

Saorla smiled. "Goodnight, Aileen."

"Goodnight, my love."

9: Father Maverick

"WELL, THAT WAS smashing." Aileen dropped the napkin onto her empty plate and picked up her tea.

"It was," Saorla agreed absently. It was coming up on nine o'clock, and she was fidgety. The service started at ten-thirty, and if Finn and Erin didn't get a move on, they'd miss their breakfast—that or be late. "Maybe they've been in already."

"Unlikely, knowing your Finn. Are you eating that?" Aileen nodded at Saorla's plate, which was still half full.

"Why? Did you want it?"

"God, no. I'm stuffed." Aileen patted her belly to prove it. She claimed she'd put on a stone and a half since they'd met, which wasn't bad going in fifty-two years, but Saorla couldn't tell. All she saw were lovely soft curves as familiar as her own reflection.

"Are you going to call your Martin again?"

"Aye, I will." Aileen took out her phone, holding it at arm's length while she located her brother's number onscreen. "I bet they're still in bed."

"Your mum and Martin?"

"Finn and Erin. Oh, here we are." She poked the screen and put the phone to her ear. "It's ringing... Hello, Martin? It's Ail— well, I know, but it's manners. Everything all right?" She paused to listen and then made eye contact with Saorla. "He's making the breakfast." Another pause. "She's not keen on boiled eggs. There's cereal in the cupboard above the stove... A fire hazard." She tutted. "Keeps it crisp, so... Whatever you think, Martin... Oh, we're fine... Full English, aye, and the hotel's grand."

Far too grand. Lace tablecloths, china service...

"All right. Don't forget her pills. There's lactulose in the fridge if—has she? Oh, well, best not give her any more, then. Love to you both. Bye now." Aileen moved her phone away and squinted at it. "He's gone."

"Everything all right?"

"So he says."

"That's good," Saorla said, although Aileen looked pensive. Her mum turned ninety in September, and she'd had a couple of strokes, but she was in reasonable health. However, it was the first time Aileen had left her brother in charge, so she was bound to worry. She was also a mistress of deflection when she didn't want to talk about something.

"So, what's bothering you? The boys?" she asked.

"Oh, I don't think there'll be trouble today."

"It's a priest doing the baptism, your Sean was saying last night."

"Former priest."

"He wasn't stripped of his duties, was he?"

"Left of his own accord, I think."

"You mean like…" Aileen clicked her fingers. "Oh, God, what was his name? The one who came after Father Corcoran."

"Father Thomas?"

"Between Corcoran and Thomas."

"The interim priest?" Saorla tried to recall, but the man had been with them only a month or two. "Mc…Mc… McCann?"

"Could've been McCullough."

"Isn't he your dentist?"

Aileen laughed at her mistake. Mr. McCullough was a good-looking man, not that he'd have Aileen going weak at the knees. "Are you sure it was Mc-something?"

"I'm not sure of anything today. What about him, anyway?"

"He resigned because of the salary scandal."

"Salary scandal… You come up with some funny ideas, Aileen Cullen."

"It's true! It was in the paper a while back. Derry priests were being paid less. Father Whatever-his-name-is was interviewed as part of the exposé and got hauled up before the bishop."

Saorla was sure Aileen was spinning her a yarn. "Did you get this from Mary Rose?" She was Mary Donnelly, really, but she did the church flowers and was always complaining she was an old wreck, so it suited. Nothing got past Mary—if it was worth knowing, she knew it. However, she could dress up her words as well as she could dress the church. "Gallagher." It came to her in a flash.

"That's not Mc-something."

"Maybe I was thinking about your dentist, too."

Aileen leaned across the table, resting her chin on her hand, and fluttered her eyelashes. "Oh, is that so?"

Saorla laughed it off. "What were we talking about?"

"I was saying this one who's doing your Dylan's baptism might've left the Church for the same kind of thing."

"Well, we'll see in—Christ, look at the time. We'd best get going." Saorla finished the last of her tea and pushed her chair out, hooking her bag from under the table with her foot before she got up.

"What about your Finn and Erin?" Aileen stole the sausage from Saorla's plate.

"If they're not ready, we'll walk." Saorla pushed her chair back in. "I thought you said you were stuffed."

"Always room for a sausage." Aileen grinned.

Saorla felt the blood rush to her cheeks. "God, you're uncouth."

Aileen took a bite of the sausage but left the rest on the plate in favour of hooking arms so they could return to their room to finish getting ready.

Finn and Erin's door opened as they passed it, and Saorla stopped—or would've done if Aileen hadn't kept pulling her onwards.

"Morning, ladies," Finn greeted with a big grin.

"Will you be ready?" Saorla called back over her shoulder.

"Sure. We'll have a piece of toast and be right with you."

"You're eating now?"

"It won't take five minutes."

"Communion within the hour."

"Nobody does..." Finn trailed off at Aileen's warning glare. "All right. I'll fetch Erin." He disappeared back into the room.

"Never argues with you, does he?" Saorla complained, but with a smile. Both lads knew better than to answer back if Aileen stepped in. It usually meant their mother was at the end of her tether. Of course, they weren't to know that sometimes it was a ploy to shut them up. Or maybe they did and decided it wasn't worth taking the chance.

Either way, it had worked a treat, as Finn and Erin were ready and waiting when Saorla and Aileen arrived downstairs a quarter of an hour later.

"Are we fit?" Erin asked, quickly followed by a gasp. "Oh, your dresses are lovely!"

"Why, thank you!" Saorla gave a half-curtsy, while Aileen fussed self-consciously. Saorla's dress was mainly blue in a chiffon-type fabric with a large butterfly print and three-quarter sleeves. She wasn't a dress kind of person, but when she'd seen it in the catalogue, she'd been quite taken with it and was pleased with how it looked and felt.

Aileen's was deep green with wide shoulder straps and a flared, knee-length skirt, much like the dresses she'd worn when they were young, with a wee flash of her knees as the fabric lifted with her movements. After all these years, it still made Saorla's heart race, and as they climbed into the back of Erin's car, she whispered, "You look beautiful."

Aileen blushed and smiled bashfully. "So do you," she whispered back. Saorla kissed Aileen's cheek, which made it glow even pinker.

"Steady now in the back," Finn said, and got flicks on both ears for his troubles.

***

"These can't all be for the baptism, surely?" Aileen was agog at the chapel's full car park, or almost full. There was one disabled space left. Since Erin had been ferrying Finn around for the past six months or more, she'd made him apply for his 'disabled' badge, but she still checked there was nobody whose need was greater before she took the space.

"You go on ahead," Finn suggested as he struggled out of the car without a single curse even though his face showed the effort. He said the physiotherapy was helping, but getting his pain under control without drugging himself to the eyeballs was a longer journey. Mostly he was better these days—thank God, because when he was bad, he was worse than ever—and it was a glimmer of hope for Saorla, that he might yet learn to live instead of simply surviving.

"We don't mind waiting, darlin'."

"It's all right," Erin assured her.

With a shrug, Saorla and Aileen walked on towards the chapel. Sean, Josh and Hay were standing outside the vast main door, in deep conversation with a man in vestments whom Saorla assumed to be the maverick priest. Josh was the first to notice and alerted Sean to their approach.

"Ah, Mum, Aunty Aileen, come and meet Father Mallick."

Saorla half-choked on her suppressed amusement as she said, "Good morning, Father."

"Good morning, Mrs. Tierney." His handshake was warm, soft and two-handed. "And Miss Cullen."

He repeated the motion with Aileen, who was doing a terrible job of hiding that she was eavesdropping on Josh and Hay's conversation.

"Let me quickly run through the order of service so you know what to expect."

Saorla nodded her consent.

"The chapel has a resident pastor, and she will begin the service as usual—"

"She?"

"Yes. Pastor Rebecca Berry. The chapel is an interdenominational place of worship, and Communion isn't a regular part of the morning prayer service. Rebecca will give her usual welcome; I will lead the baptism, followed by Communion."

Saorla considered whether she should say what was on her mind. It was disrespectful to question a member of the clergy, never mind that he'd referred to another member of the clergy by their first name in front of non-clergy.

"I sense you have reservations, Mrs. Tierney."

She looked the man over, noting the gentle smile above a clean-shaven chin, the short, neat hair and the sincere deep-brown eyes. "Forgive me, Father, if this seems impertinent, but... are you qualified to administer the Eucharist?"

Father Mallick's smile broadened. "We are all priests in God's kingdom."

Oh, we've got ourselves a comedian. Saorla pursed her lips, unimpressed. His face soon straightened.

"But, of course, that's not what you're asking, Mrs. Tierney. I no longer have sacerdotal authority within the Roman Catholic Church."

"You're a layperson?"

"In the eyes of Rome, yes."

"Right. So, did you jump or were you pushed?"

"That's a matter of opinion, on which my wife and I differ. Perhaps, after we have baptised your grandson, you'll permit me to explain."

10: Bí Thusa Mo Shúile

*H*IS WIFE?" AILEEN hissed as the pair of them scurried inside. "That's what the man said." Saorla kept her sights on Dylan's present antics of trotting after the triplets as they toured the tiny chapel.

"Oh, this is beautiful," Aileen exclaimed and slowed to a virtual stop as she gazed around her and up into the rafters; she'd have walked into the end of a pew had Saorla not steered her back on track.

Saorla hadn't taken much notice of what the place looked like from the outside, beyond it being an old building, and her prior expectations had been shaped by that word people kept using: *interdenominational*. No doubt that meant all kinds of funny ideas about praising God, although Saorla didn't have a problem with Protestants. It would've been a poor do when so many good friends of theirs had been in the Order. She'd never told Cian that, of course.

But she had to agree with Aileen; the chapel was beautiful. The ornate stained-glass window in the sanctuary depicted Christ on the cross, and the altar bore silver Communion vessels and a crucifix. There was a low pulpit to the right, and the white marble font was mere feet from where they stood. Interdenominational or otherwise, this was God's house, and Saorla's soul resonated the same joy and reverence she felt in her own church.

A waving hand rose from a pew to their left. Without knowing whose hand it was, Saorla moved towards it, relieved to find, once she was close enough, it belonged to Sophie, who was smiling as if all was well and a disgraced priest wasn't baptising her son.

"Good morning. Did you sleep well?"

"I…yes, thank you, Sophie." She hadn't, because she'd been too caught up thinking about the baptism and wishing she'd been more forthright last night in asking Josh and Hay how they intended to fulfil their godparenting duties, considering Josh was a non-believer and Hay was a pagan, or something along those lines. "How about you?"

"Not bad—between Sean's snoring and Dylan singing along with the dawn chorus."

"Ah, yes." Saorla nodded knowingly. "If he's anything like his father, he'll grow out of it just in time for starting school, and then you'll be fighting to get him out of his bed rather than trying to keep him in it."

Sophie laughed but was pulled up short by the sudden cessation in happy noise, followed by Dylan's instantly identifiable wailing. The triplets about-turned and gasped in unison before running back the way they had come. The non-identical one—Sage—ducked out of sight, reappearing a second later with Dylan in her arms. She hurried through the pews towards them, and the red blur—all Saorla could see without her glasses—showed itself to be a bleeding nose.

Sophie groaned, and muttered, "He couldn't have timed that better if he'd tried." She edged past Saorla and took Dylan from Sage.

"He tripped over, Sophie. He was running after us and… he just tripped over." The poor girl was devastated and on the brink of tears, and Sophie was in too much of a state to offer the reassurance she needed.

"Oh, don't you worry," Saorla comforted, glancing around for the girl's mother, who must still have been outside with Josh and Father Maver…*Mallick*. Saorla put her arm around Sage's shoulders and bent a little to say, "They do it all the time at this age, especially when they're excited. I'm sure you were the same yourself."

Sage nodded uncertainly and peered around Saorla to where Sophie wasn't doing so well at consoling her son.

"Good mor..." a man's voice began jovially. Saorla didn't recognise it and turned to find a middle-aged man and woman stopped in the aisle and staring in horror.

"What on earth's happened?" the woman asked.

"Fallen over and bashed his nose," Sophie answered wearily. She tugged another wad of tissues from her bag and held it under Dylan's chin to catch the drips. "Saorla, this is Bonnie and Derek—my mum and dad. Mum, Dad, this is Saorla—Sean's mum—and her friend Aileen."

"I could tell as soon as I saw you," Bonnie said, stepping closer to Saorla. Sage backed off to give the two women room to lightly hug and kiss cheeks. "It's lovely to meet you finally."

"And you," Saorla said, accepting the same greeting from Derek before they moved on to Aileen, who seemed delightfully overwhelmed by everything.

At first glance, Sophie looked like neither parent, though there were recognisable features here and there, like the high brows, which had caused Saorla some consternation initially, convinced Sophie was worrying all the time. Those were definitely inherited from her father, while her heart-shaped face and colouring—hair like dark caramel and ivory skin—came from her mother.

"Look at his gown," Sophie lamented.

"It's only a few spots," her mum reasoned.

"It'll stain." Poor Sophie sounded like she might burst into tears herself at any given moment—understandably.

Saorla had offered to make Dylan's baptism gown; she still had Finn and Sean's, but they'd been tiny babes, and it was nowhere near big enough. Sophie told her not to worry, as she still had her own baptism gown, and Saorla had been disappointed, but she had to admit it was lovely, and it could almost have been made for him, though it was a wee bit long, and probably why he'd tripped over.

"What are you doing, cheeky?" Bonnie smiled at Dylan. He scowled and snuggled in tighter against Sophie's shoulder. At least his nose had stopped bleeding.

"What a grouchy face," Saorla cooed, to no effect. She met Bonnie's gaze, both knowing it was hopeless trying to cheer the wee man up; he was already in the best place.

If nothing else, the kerfuffle had distracted Saorla from her woes long enough for the pastor to have arrived. The woman glanced over the growing congregation with a smile before turning away to kneel at the altar in prayer for a few moments, during which Sean, Josh, Hay, Finn, Erin and a few more joined them. The two pews in front filled with people Saorla didn't know, yet all of whom acknowledged her.

There was no procession, and the congregation continued their quiet murmur as the pastor rose from the altar rail and took up a position that suggested she was ready when they were. Saorla was surprised by how unconcerned she was for the lack of formality, although Sean was fussing.

"What's the matter?" she asked.

"I'm fine," he fibbed. "Are you all right?"

She narrowed her eyes. "I'm fine, too. Sit down, darlin'."

He did as she suggested, scanning their pew and the one in front. Finn was directly in front of Saorla, Erin next to him. The woman to Erin's left was looking over her shoulder and mouthed the word 'later' at Sean.

Stunning red hair, green eyes, freckles—Saorla had heard her described so often and in such detail that she just knew the woman was Sean's friend, Shaunna.

Shaunna made eye contact with Saorla and smiled, but the organ had stopped, and so she turned to face front again, treating those behind her to a mesmerising view of her long, fiery locks.

The pastor stepped forward to address her flock. "Hello, everyone. It's so good to see you all on this bright, sunny Sunday. We have a very special service this morning. We're here to celebrate and give thanks for Dylan." She looked to where they were sitting. "Welcome, all of you. That's quite a supporters' club you have there, young man."

A low murmur of amusement rippled through the small congregation whose number was about double what it would have been without friends and family there for the baptism.

The pastor continued, "Sophie and Sean want to share their joy with all of you this morning. I'm joined by Father Mallick, whom many of you know already. Father Mallick will lead us for Dylan's baptism and, for those of you who receive it, Holy Communion. Let us pray."

Saorla slid forward and noticed Aileen do the same. They both dipped their heads and pretended they hadn't been looking for kneelers; everyone else had remained seated. Then came the shock of the unfamiliar words, which was no bad thing. It wasn't as if Saorla mindlessly went through the motions every Sunday, but there were certainly times when she prayed and chanted and listened without ever connecting her thoughts to her actions. She closed her eyes and focused solely on the pastor's words.

"Daily we live side by side. We care and provide for our families, enjoying their love and companionship. Our kin bring us great joy, and we give thanks for their health and happiness. Yet sometimes, we become caught up in our own lives, and forget about those in our community who face great hardship.

"Let us bring to mind those without homes; those who have lost loved ones; those who are unwell, or are unable to care for and provide for themselves."

The pastor stopped speaking to allow a few moments of silence: a time for private prayer and reflection.

Saorla brought before God all those who needed His guidance, or whom she hoped He would show mercy. Finn and Sean were always in there, of course. Today, so were Josh and Hay, who would soon commit to taking care of Dylan's spiritual well-being, though neither could have been a godparent had this been a real Catholic baptism. Still, Saorla had trusted Josh to care for her own son, and while she didn't know Hay well enough to pass judgement, Sean and Sophie would do what was best for Dylan... other than hemming his baptism gown.

"This morning, let us make a commitment to care for and support not only those known to us, but also our wider community.

"May our spirits be blessed with insight, our actions with understanding and compassion. May our personal faiths bring us strength and honesty.

"Amen."

The congregation responded, "Amen."

"Our first hymn this morning is one we haven't sung here before, I believe?" The pastor addressed the three young people on their way to the front with a guitar, a fiddle and a cajón.

The guitarist nodded at the pastor as she and her fellow musicians took up position next to the pulpit. While that was happening, the pastor pointed a remote control up towards the centre of the chapel. After a bit of checking they were in tune, the cajón player tapped out a rhythm; the guitar came in, and then the fiddle: 'Be Thou My Vision'.

Saorla gasped and covered her mouth with her hand, although the accompaniment disguised her surprise from all but those nearby—or her surprise at the choice of hymn, at any rate, as once again, she and Aileen were thrown by the unexpected when both moved to stand and quickly sat back.

"Nobody's getting up," Aileen muttered, fussing with Bible in the back of the pew in front. "And where's the choir?"

"I think they're wanting us to sing." Saorla indicated the screen that had descended in front of the sanctuary, onto which the words were projected.

Sean leaned forward to whisper, "You don't have to if you don't want."

Saorla nodded her understanding and smiled, determined not to cry, because it was silly, but it was her favourite hymn, one they'd sung often in school. It had been sung a few times in church, too—in English and Irish. She knew both versions, but few people sang in church back home, and she was blessed only with the will, not the ability, so she quietly let herself be taken over by the voices all around, some high, some low, some tuneful, some less so.

Slane was the first thing Sean had learned to play on the fiddle, or the first he'd learned to play well, and in no way discernible as the tune 'Be Thou My Vision' was set to until they'd endured a few months of tuneless sawing. He'd eventually mastered the thing, albeit as a hobby; he was always more into his books than his music. If he'd wanted to take it further, she'd have found a way to pay for lessons, but she was thankful he hadn't. It was enough of a stretch forking out for replacement strings, even if his need for them did decrease as he improved, unlike Finn's need for football boots. She was sure the lad's feet had grown a size bigger every week.

Aileen had paid for a few pairs along the way, and dismissed Saorla's offers to repay, saying, 'They're as good as my children, it's the least I can do.' And here she was, as always, at Saorla's side, happily singing away. She'd been in the choir when she was younger and still had a lovely voice, so sweet and melodic. It was all kinds of wrong what 'Bí Thusa Mo Shúile' from that woman's lips did to Saorla...though it had to be said, when Aileen was in full swing, she could outdo the vacuum cleaner.

Aileen must've sensed Saorla's eyes on her, because she turned and smiled as she sang the Irish, not English, "Is tabhair domsa áit cónaí, Istigh i do chroí."

Give me a place to live, inside your heart.

What a terrible, wonderful woman she was.

11: In the Name of Every Blessed Thing

WE COME TOGETHER this morning to celebrate a new life. We are indeed blessed that a child is born into this world in innocence and love, a tiny human dependent on us all—family and community—for his nourishment and nurture.

"We all share in the joy of Dylan's life, as we all share the responsibility to love and care for him over the years ahead. Of course, Dylan is a young child now, not a baby, but this morning, we formally welcome him and bestow his name.

"Dylan Robert was born on the twenty-fourth of August almost two years ago, and unlike Dad, he arrived right on time."

At that, all of those in the back three pews burst into laughter, including Sean, who turned red as a tomato.

"Luckily, Mum knows what Dad's like, and Uncle George was on hand."

George and Josh were giggling like a pair of schoolboys, but they soon caught themselves on when Father Mallick began moving down the aisle towards them, still addressing the congregation as a whole.

"Now, a name—" he stopped walking and rotated on the spot, all eyes following his motion "—is very important." He nodded ponderously, quite the entertainer, and then continued on his way. "It's important because it distinguishes each of us and gives us a sense of belonging in our family and community.

"Dylan's name also indicates the strength and importance of his Irish and English heritage." He drew level with the third pew from the back and scanned the faces of everyone there for the baptism, pausing when he reached Saorla. His smile was a question: *will you trust me to do God's work?*

For several long seconds, she looked him dead in the eye; he neither flinched nor looked away. Whatever troubles he'd had with the Church were behind him, so confident was he that he could do the deed.

Saorla nodded once, and Father Mallick responded in kind before turning on his heel to continue his address.

"Dylan's baptism is a little different, as Sophie and Sean are keen to ensure their son follows a path of his own choosing, but they, and the guardians they have chosen, will make promises to love and protect Dylan, and to guide him through life in the best ways they know."

Crouching low next to Sophie—she'd stayed by the aisle, with Dylan sitting on her knee, in case his nose started bleeding again—Father Mallick extended his hand to Dylan and said, "Hiya. Shall we have a wash in the special water, get some of this yucky mess off?"

Saorla couldn't see the wee man's face as he looked to his mum for reassurance. Sophie smiled and released her hold on him, and just like that, Dylan stretched his arms up to the priest.

Father Mallick smiled and picked him up. "You're looking *very* smart today," he said to Dylan, then, in a slightly louder voice, "Sophie, Sean, Hay and Josh, please will you join me?" The four of them rose and followed the priest to the font. "If anyone here for Dylan wishes to move closer, please do."

"Shall we?" Aileen whispered.

Saorla looked to see what Sophie's mum and dad thought. They were already up on their feet and edging along the pew. Saorla and Aileen stepped aside and let Bonnie and Derek lead the way. As they drew near the font, Aileen's hand shot up in front of Saorla's face.

"Oh, God. Don't look."

"Aileen!" Saorla shoved her hand away. "Oh!"

There was a rubber duck taking a swim in the holy water, under the power of Dylan's splashing; Father Mallick carried on, regardless.

"Jesus called the little children to Him and said, 'Suffer the little children to come unto me, and forbid them not; for of such is the kingdom of God.' In this manner of ever-abiding love, we enter into baptism as an affirmation of God's presence.

"Sophie and Sean, you have brought your son in the presence of friends and loved ones to celebrate the expression of his eternal life. You have appointed Hay and Josh as guardians for this child. Is this correct?" Father Mallick blinked as a particularly large splash hit him in the face.

The parents and godparents—or whatever name they were going by—pretended they hadn't noticed and answered, "Yes."

"Will you, Sophie and Sean as parents, and Hay and Josh as guardians, teach this child that he has the right to life and love?"

"We will."

"Will you offer Dylan a broad and balanced view of life, and encourage in him the virtues of integrity, honesty, love and fairness towards his fellow human beings?"

"We will."

"Hay and Josh, will you be a shoulder for Sophie and Sean to lean on whenever they need it, and be there as second parents when called upon?"

"We will."

"Sophie and Sean, please confirm what you have named this child."

"Dylan Robert."

Father Mallick reached around Dylan and dipped his fingers in the water then pressed them to Dylan's forehead, somehow keeping them in place as Dylan turned and gave him a very stern frown.

"Dylan Robert, I baptise you in the name of the Father, the Son and the Holy Ghost. May your life be surrounded with God's love, and the love of all the people who welcome you here today."

That was all it took: one mention of the Trinity, and Saorla finally let go of the worries she'd carried ever since Sean told her Dylan was to be baptised. Now she thought reasonably about it, it hadn't been much different from other baptisms she'd attended—aside from the duck.

Father Mallick lifted Dylan away from the font and gave him to Sophie, who immediately gave him to Hay. The adoring way she smiled down at him left Saorla more certain than ever that she would be a perfect godmother-thingy.

"Welcome, Dylan, to our family and to our hearts. Bear your name with honour, for it is your name, and it is powerful." She lifted him as high above her head as her arms would allow, hoisting her tremendous, free breasts several inches upwards. "We ask the gods to watch over you, and we wish your family love and light."

All right, maybe not *quite* perfect.

At Saorla's side, Aileen was lost in a daze, and continued to stare up in the air after Hay was done chanting, and the congregation had stopped applauding, and Dylan had been passed on to Josh. God only knew what the poor mite was in for next.

Josh held him at arm's length and studied him for a moment.

"Oshy," Dylan shouted and wriggled to break free. "Down, please."

Josh raised an eyebrow. "We'll talk later," he said, and handed him off to Sean.

"Thank you, all," Father Mallick said, confirming the baptism was complete.

"Come on," Saorla prompted and hooked Aileen around the middle, shifting her aside to let past those who'd been sitting further from the aisle.

"That was very…" Aileen began but never finished.

"Aye," Saorla agreed. It was certainly very *something*. She wasn't sure what.

The rest of the service was quite ordinary, by comparison. Father Mallick administered the Eucharist in the Catholic tradition; they sang another hymn—'O Jesus I Have Promised'—to a very modern and completely unsingable tune, although again, the musicians played beautifully. Then came the closing prayers and the Grace.

Saorla had never been so delighted to be sitting near the door. She was exhausted, and yet, as she stepped out into the warm June sunshine, her spirit felt lighter than it had in a long, long time.

12: A Gathering

"**R**IGHT, MUM. PUT that kettle down."

"I don't mind, darlin'. You're busy."

"I'm waiting to do the introductions."

"Oh, right."

It was a fine day, warm and sunny, and a fair few had come back from the chapel. With Sean's house being so small, everyone was out in the garden—apart from Aileen and Erin, who'd stopped off at the hotel, and Dylan, who'd had a dose of paracetamol syrup and gone to nap.

Ignoring Sean's impatient sigh, Saorla finished filling the kettle and got it back onto its stand before she allowed him to lead her outside, where the conversations continued but with a few sideways glances in their direction.

"I thought your brother was out here."

"He went with Erin and Aileen."

Aileen had said she needed to 'freshen up', which meant she needed to use the toilet, and she'd said she'd walk back from the hotel, but Erin wouldn't hear of it. As for Finn—he could rest his leg at Sean's as well as any place. "He'd better not ditch the party," Saorla said.

"It's not really a party, is it? And if he doesn't want to be here—"

"He can make the effort for one day of his life." Saorla quickly painted a smile over her muttering as she neared the dozen or so people standing and sitting around the patio table.

"Right, who don't you know?" Sean wasn't really asking her; he was thinking aloud. "OK, so, everyone, this is my mum,

Saorla. Mum, this is Margita." He lightly touched the shoulder of a demure, grey-haired woman in a floral two-piece suit. Her head jerked as she turned, startled to see who was behind her. "Margita's our fantastic admin saviour at the university. The place would grind to a standstill without her."

"Hello," Margita greeted, mouselike, eyes flitting every which way. Saorla thought Sean was rotten making the poor woman go first.

"Lovely to meet you," she responded, unsure what else to say—*so, you're an administrator? That's...exciting*—but Sean quickly moved along.

"You know Joshy and George—has Lib gone home?"

"Gone to meet Poppy off the bus," George said.

Sean nodded his understanding but didn't explain who Poppy was, so Saorla assumed she didn't need to know.

"And this is Aitch." Sean gestured as a tall man stepped around the table to take Saorla's hand.

"Hello, Mrs. Tierney."

He had a dashing smile, though the scar and shaved head, coupled with the size of him, made him look a bit of a thug, even if he was in his Sunday best.

"Saorla, please," she beseeched. He cranked up the dazzle factor a few notches. Saorla swooned a little; she had a soft spot for ruffians. "Why the nickname, if you don't mind me asking, Aitch?"

"Not at all. My name's Henry Hartley, and everyone used to call me Aitch-Aitch, but it was too much of a mouthful, apparently."

"Right." Saorla chuckled.

"Aitch is a detective inspector in the police, Mum."

"Is that so?" She hadn't been far off, then.

"For my sins."

A loud 'ha' sounded from Josh. "I still can't believe you're a good Catholic boy, Aitch."

"Who said anything about good?" Aitch winked at Saorla. "There's always confession, eh?"

She got a bit flustered, helped not at all by the next introduction, because there was definitely more going on here than met the eye.

"This is Shaunna," Sean said, but Shaunna was already up and leaning in for a hug and kiss. Red curls tickled Saorla's nose, and she tried to subtly puff them out of the way, but sniffed instead. The smell was as intoxicating as the vision.

"It's so lovely to meet you, Saorla. Sean talks about you all the time."

"All the time?" Saorla asked. Her voice sounded too loud and quivery next to Shaunna's soft cheek.

"When he's not talking about himself." Shaunna withdrew and cast a sultry smile Sean's way.

"I'm as modest as they come," he protested, which sent everyone into reels of laughter. Shaunna squeezed his arm and mouthed *just kidding*. Sean's answering smile confirmed Saorla's suspicions, and if he hadn't been flirting back, Sean might just have noticed he wasn't the only one taken with the beautiful redhead. She really was lovely.

Once the rabble died down, Sean finished off his introductions. "This is Eleanor, who you already know."

Eleanor nodded and smiled. "Hello, again."

"Hello, Eleanor. Good to see you. You're looking well."

"Thanks. You, too."

'Know' was putting it a bit strongly. Last time Saorla had been over, she'd wanted to go to Mass, but Sean had been working, and she hadn't wanted to go on her own. He'd called Eleanor, and they'd gone together, although they'd done little more than sit next to each other for the duration and then gone their separate ways.

With the introductions made—the others present were Sophie and her mum and dad, and Hay and her three terrors—Saorla asked, "Who'd like a cup of tea?"

Sean sighed dramatically. "What did I say?"

"Hey, it might be your son's baptism, but don't forget who you're talking to." She gave him a playful nudge so he knew she was teasing, or partly teasing. He was a terrible show-off in front of people.

"That's you told," Sophie said, laughing at Sean's sulky expression. "But you sit, Saorla, and we'll make the tea. There's some wine and beer as well, if anybody fancies it?"

"Is it too early for wine?" Shaunna asked, tapping her lush lips with a fingertip and rolling her eyes skyward.

"Never," Saorla answered, too quickly.

Shaunna laughed and leaned in again to murmur, "I will if you will."

Lovely and a shocking flirt, which eased Saorla's guilt at her attraction to a woman who had to be thirty years younger than her. She'd been looking forward to a cup of tea, but... "Sure. Why not? The wee man's only going to be baptised the once."

"It's red," Sophie said.

Shaunna nodded. "Works for me."

"That's fine, Soph," Saorla confirmed, hoping she wouldn't regret it later. She glanced around the table, looking for somewhere to sit.

"Have my chair," George offered and was up out of it.

"Again?"

George shrugged. "I don't mind standing. Actually...I could bring some of ours," he suggested to Josh.

"Good idea. I'll give you a—"

"Stay there." George strode off.

Josh watched him leave and relaxed back into his seat. "I'll stay here, then." He indicated George's vacant seat. Saorla accepted his invitation.

"Bossy, isn't he?" she said.

Josh laughed and winced. "Only when he needs to be."

Saorla patted his hand. "How are you doing now? All right?" She didn't know all of the ins and outs, beyond Josh having been in hospital at the same time as Finn.

"More or less, thank you. Oh, more people…" He glanced past her towards the back door of the house. Sure enough, Aileen, Finn and Erin had arrived, but Saorla had got the message, and she had no wish to pry, even if it meant never fully understanding why Sean put Josh's well-being above his own brother's.

13: Trouble

AILEEN STUCK HER head out the door and gave everyone a wave before disappearing back inside. Saorla half-considered going in herself, just to watch Sean trying to talk Aileen out of helping with the tea, but then Finn stopped in front of her, blocking her view. She leaned back and squinted up at him. He'd been in a fine mood all morning, but he was in a stinker of one now if the snarl was any measure. "What's the matter with your face?"

He waved his crutch in the direction of the house. "Some tube in a Yank tank's taking up half the road. We had to park miles away."

Erin sighed. "No, we didn't."

"That'll be Andy," Shaunna said, already on the move. "I'll get him to park somewhere else."

"It's all ri...." Saorla began, but it was too late. Shaunna had gone. With a weary shake of the head, Erin followed her, stepping aside to let George through with a stack of garden chairs. He smiled his thanks as they passed.

"I've just brought four for now." He dumped them next to the table and unstacked them. "Hi, Finn. You OK?"

"Fine, thanks. Yourself?"

"Yeah, same." George placed one of the chairs behind Finn and another on Josh's other side.

"I can move," Saorla offered.

"It's OK," George assured her and sat down. "Andy's here," he told Josh.

"So I believe." Josh cast a cool glance Finn's way, but Finn was preoccupied with settling into his chair and didn't see it.

"Isn't Andy Shaunna's…" Saorla didn't know what to call him, and wouldn't have said anything at all but for the atmosphere brewing. All this time, she'd been worried about Sean and Finn kicking off; she hadn't expected trouble from Josh.

"Yeah, it is," George confirmed with a frown. "What is he? Boyfriend, I guess. It doesn't seem right calling him that. Baby daddy?"

"Babies," Josh corrected. "But that implies they're no longer together." He turned to Saorla. "They are still together, incidentally."

"Oh, right. So how about…" Saorla searched for the term, or any words at all. It was surely her paranoia, not Josh warning her off. "Common-law husband?" she suggested.

Josh nodded noncommittally and then jumped, as did they all, at the racket of Erin's keys hitting the tabletop. She glared furiously at Finn, whose innocent shrug didn't appease her in the slightest.

"Oh, my goodness, look at those curls!" Saorla gushed, latterly realising she couldn't have timed a distraction more perfectly, but it was an honest reaction to the sight of the babe in—she presumed—Andy's arms. Red hair, unmistakeably her mother's child, whilst her twin sister—in Shaunna's arms—was dark-haired like her dad. Now there was a family blessed with the good-looking genes.

"Who wants 'em?" Andy asked as he neared the table.

Saorla had the urge to stick her hand in the air and shout 'Me! Me! Me!' but she didn't need to. Shaunna sidestepped Finn to get close enough for Saorla to take the baby from her.

"God, she's gorgeous. Look at her. Hello there!"

"This is Sorsha," Shaunna said. Andy had passed the other twin to George. "And that's Rosie."

"Well, hello, Sorsha." The wee girl blinked big brown eyes, and Saorla's grandmotherly instincts went haywire. "How old are you, then?"

"Nearly one," Shaunna answered on her daughter's behalf.

"It's nearly your first birthday? Well, isn't that grand!"

At the word 'birthday', Sorsha broke into coos and smiles that dimpled her chubby cheeks.

Shaunna beamed down at her daughters, as besotted as any mother, then sighed and shook her head. "I can't believe it's here already. It's gone so fast."

"Aye, it does," Saorla empathised. She caught sight of the other twin copying her mummy's actions, the both of them shaking their heads in turn, those gorgeous red curls bouncing all over the show. Laughing, Saorla turned her attention back to Sorsha, who was quietly watching, laid back and content, and for a moment, looking down on that head of curly brown-black hair, it was Sean on Saorla's knee. He'd been a good baby, so long as he was kept well fed and got his quota of sleep in—yet another way Dylan took after his dad.

The spell was broken by Rosie babbling loudly. She reached for her sister, and they touched fingertips, both giggling in delight.

"They've got that twin connection, I see," Saorla remarked.

"Yeah. We're gonna have our work cut out for us when they start school."

"I know that feeling. Not quite the same, I know, but my two were thick as thieves, even in their teens." Or the two years their teens coincided—the two years before Finn's accident—when they'd fought like mad things at home, but away from it, they'd stuck by each other, come what may.

For all their mischief—and it would only have got worse—Saorla would've given anything to turn back time. If she'd stopped Finn going out that night…but why would she? It had been a nice evening, and he was a decent driver, or as decent as any nineteen-year-old lad could be. And there'd been no premonitions, no woman's intuition; she couldn't have known. Yet the questions still came, unbidden: *What if I'd made him do the dishes before he left? What if that guy had left work on time?* It wouldn't have just saved Finn's suffering.

"They're nothing like each other personality-wise." If Shaunna had said it because she'd noticed Saorla's mind drifting, she didn't let on. "Rosie's sunshine and showers. Mostly showers. And don't you dare say like her mother." She stretched an arm behind her and poked Andy's midriff.

"Didn't even think it," he claimed, though the cheeky smirk cast some doubt on his sincerity.

Moody or no, Rosie was all sunshine right then, and completely enthralled by all the people coming—Sean and Sophie with the drinks—and going—Hay taking the triplets to the park to burn off some of the energy they'd accumulated at the chapel. With the pink cheeks and vibrant hair, exactly the same shade as her mother's, Rosie's name couldn't have been more perfect.

"Sorsha's not a name I've heard before," Saorla thought aloud.

"Yeah, it's Irish but not quite," Shaunna said with a laugh. "Long story, but the short version is my eldest daughter chose it."

"Oh, right. That's Krissi, isn't it?"

"Erm…yeah." Shaunna's gaze drifted to Sean, who was talking to the men but immediately stopped yattering and looked her way.

"What's up?"

"You've left us nothing to talk about."

"Sorry?" Sean was clueless.

"See, that's exactly what I meant about social networks," Josh said, prompting multiple groans from around the table.

"They weren't talking about social networks," Eleanor pointed out.

"It's the same principle," Josh argued. "Where's the joy in catching up with an old friend if they already know everything you've done since the last time you saw each other?"

"We've never met before," Shaunna said. "Although it feels like we have." She tugged a large handbag across the table and searched inside. "Are you online, Saorla?"

"I am."

"Awesome." Shaunna withdrew her phone from the bag and, reading the screen with enviable ease, tapped it a few times before announcing, "Friend request sent."

"What's that?" Aileen put a glass of wine on the table in front of Saorla. "This is for you, I believe?"

"It is. Thanks."

"But you don't drink red."

"There wasn't any white. I don't mind red, anyway."

"Hmm." Aileen turned her nose up.

"Here, Aunty Aileen." Sean placed one of the remaining chairs next to Saorla's.

"Oh, thank you, Sean. Very kind." With tea in hand, Aileen sat and eyed Saorla's wine with suspicion, then did the same with Shaunna's.

"So, Josh," Finn said, a definite challenge in his tone, "how can an atheist make the promises you did this morning?"

"I made no promises I couldn't keep."

"Surely, as a spiritual guardian—"

"Philosophical guardian," Josh contended.

"So…what, you're going to teach the wee lad all about Pythagoras?"

"He was a mathematician, not a philosopher," Sean interjected. Saorla didn't care for his tone much, either.

"He was a philosopher, too," Josh said, gazing steadily at Finn. "You know about philosophy?"

"Bits and pieces, aye. Plenty of time to read. You know I mean?"

Josh nodded dolefully. "Yes, I do."

"Right, so, with all your reading, you'll have read the Bible."

"Several times over."

"So how can you be sure there's no God?"

"I can't, not one hundred percent. But in terms of probability…"

"Oh, now you're talking my language." Finn sat forward, elbows on the table. "Have you heard of Bayes Law?"

"It's a theorem, but yes, I have."

"A theorem, you say…"

14: Strife

WHILE FINN AND Josh parried words, Saorla sipped her wine and did her best to tune them out, instead watching Sorsha's inquisitive expression—a delicate frown, sparse rapid blinks all the more noticeable for her thick dark lashes—as she listened to the heated but mercifully civil debate. No doubt it made about as much sense to the wee girl as it did to Saorla.

She always underestimated Finn's intellect. Everyone did, assuming Sean was the clever one, but both boys had left school with a decent set of qualifications. The difference was that Sean loved learning, whereas Finn just wanted a job and money in his pocket, and the only taxing his brain got voluntarily was calculating odds and returns, or so Saorla had thought, but listening to him, he'd clearly been having them all on.

"Do you want me to take her?"

"Hmm?" Saorla only half heard Shaunna's question, but she fully caught Sean's reproachful glower at his brother before he covered it with a smile and started a conversation with Andy. "You're all right, unless you want to?"

Shaunna held up her free hand. "No, no. You carry on." She smiled, a flash of perfect white teeth, her lips parting wider as she turned when Sophie called her name. Andy's arm snaked around Shaunna's waist in what seemed an instinctive gesture of affection, or maybe even possessiveness, and Saorla could fully appreciate why. Everything about the woman was so vibrant and tactile, from the soft red curls, meticulously made-up green eyes and glossy lips, to the smooth curves of her generous hour-glass figure.

Aileen's shoulder bumped Saorla's. "D'you remember my hair being like that?"

Saorla smiled. "I do." Up until her forties, Aileen's hair had been down to her waist, usually kept in a plait twisted into a bun, to stop it turning to frizz. It had been as bright as Shaunna's, though more a deep orange than red.

After the cancer in her forties—she'd been clear since, thank God—her hair had grown back grey, whether due to the stress or the chemotherapy, it was impossible to say. The doctor insisted it was Aileen's age and she'd have gone grey anyway—perhaps she hadn't noticed if she'd been dying it? Aileen was deeply offended by the question; she'd never dyed her hair in her life.

These days, it was cropped very short and a dark, almost charcoal grey. No matter how often Saorla told her it suited her, and that she was beautiful, Aileen dismissed it with a joke about the chemo granting her the superpower of a magnetic head—*it's not hair, it's iron filings.* It could've stripped her permanently bald for all Saorla cared; what mattered was Aileen hadn't been taken from her.

Maybe that was the reason for Aileen's coolness—the reminder Shaunna's hair presented—rather than jealousy. Sure, Shaunna was one of the most beautiful women Saorla had ever set eyes on, but the greater part of it was that she looked a lot like Aileen had in her younger years—all the more reason for Saorla to behave herself. It wasn't meaningless flirting if it hurt the woman she loved.

Alas, the disharmony only worsened as the afternoon went on. Aileen made idle chitchat with Eleanor and George, fully turning her back on Saorla when she accepted a wine top-up from Shaunna. Sophie and Erin brought sandwiches out and dumped them on the table with as much clattering as was possible without breaking anything, while Finn and Josh's discussion continued unabated and Sean's face was so red it was heading towards purple.

Hay and the triplets returned, all fairly worn out, which was a blessing. Any more noise on top of the chatter, the banging, the clanging of wind chimes coming from the next-door garden and Rosie getting fractious, and Saorla may very well have lost her mind.

Libby should also have returned but hadn't, and Josh and George left to investigate; Shaunna, Andy and the twins departed soon after. The others had already gone, leaving only the Tierneys and Hay's bunch.

And all the while, Dylan slept on.

"I suppose we should be getting back soon," Saorla said. She'd hoped to see more of her grandson before they left, but she was attempting a pre-emptive strike—she'd spotted Sean homing in on Finn—and it failed.

"Why the hell did you ask him that?" Sean demanded.

Finn looked Sean over, his expression unreadable even to Saorla. "I was just making conversation."

"Aye, right. Challenging him on his atheism in a garden full of Catholics? D'you think I came up the Foyle in a bubble?"

Finn laughed, though his eyes were blazing. "See, Erin? I told you we shouldn't have bothered."

Whatever Erin's thoughts, she wisely kept them to herself.

"You could've talked to him about anything at all," Sean argued.

"I know nothing about the man."

"Then you should've kept it shut. But you had to ruin it for everyone."

"For who, Sean?" Finn got to his feet with surprising agility and took a step—not closer, but away, so he was out of Sean's space. "You ready?" he asked Erin. She nodded. "We'll see you later, Mum. Aunty Aileen. Thanks, Soph."

Sophie forced out a smile. "Thank you both for coming."

With one last swift nod at Sean, Finn walked ahead of Erin, towards the house. As they reached the back door, Sean shouted, "Is that you, then?"

Finn stopped but kept his back to his brother.

"Sean," Saorla warned.

"No, Mum. He came here, to my house, and tried to start a fight with my friend. And he thinks he can just walk away, same as always."

"Jesus Christ, Sean," Finn hissed. "How old are ye?" With a bit of a struggle but no less haste, Finn surmounted the backdoor step and disappeared from view.

"Say it to my face," Sean hollered.

"No!" That was Finn's final word on the matter. The click of his crutch continued a few seconds more, then the front door slammed shut.

Sean was raging, and Saorla would've taken him on, but he looked ready to blow a gasket, and she was terrified he was going to do himself damage. Aileen had no such compunction.

"Are you done making a show of yourself?"

"Hey, I wasn't the one who—"

"Made an effort to socialise?"

"He picked an argument."

"You're wrong, but so what if he did? Your man Josh didn't rise to it."

"That's beside the point."

"Is it?"

Sean opened and closed his mouth a few times, unusually lost for words, and grunted his frustration.

"Anyone want a cup of tea?" Sophie asked. She dashed off without waiting for an answer.

"Or a tote on this?" Hay offered, holding up a lit joint.

"Is that legal in England, then?" Aileen asked.

Hay blew out a dense cloud of smoke. "Not exactly."

"Oh." Aileen looked like she might be considering it. Saorla was tempted herself. What a day it had turned out to be.

"The police turn a blind eye to personal use, Aunty Aileen," Sean explained wearily. He was calming down, thank God. He slumped into a chair and sat awhile at peace before finally, he sighed and said, "I'm sorry, Mummy."

Saorla waited to see what he was apologising for.

"He just makes me so mad—the way he acts like he's done us all a favour by coming."

"He's trying, darlin'."

"He's trying? He didn't even talk to me."

"D'ye blame him?"

Sean's brows drew together in a troubled frown. "I'm trying, too, you know. I just wish…" He never finished the sentence. There was no need when it was what they all wished.

***

Saorla and Aileen opted for dinner in the hotel restaurant, which wasn't cheap, but they were both shattered, and Saorla had a post-wine headache she was trying to conceal. Finn and Erin had gone off sightseeing and to sample the local brew, their wee fallout earlier seemingly forgotten, although Finn was still going on about Sean's poor attitude as they'd left.

"I suppose I should be grateful they didn't come to blows," Saorla said dubiously.

"I don't know," Aileen mused. "It might've cleared the air between them."

"Aye, you might be right there. They haven't had a real barney since they were kids." Saorla sighed heavily. "I've no idea what to do."

"Why should you do anything? You've stood between them long enough, my love. It's on them now."

"It's not that easy, Aileen. Doesn't matter if they're grown men. You never stop being their mother."

Aileen bristled but attempted to hide it by digging into her dessert, even though she'd been complaining she'd eaten too much.

Saorla was immediately repentant. "I'm sorry. I didn't mean that the way it came out."

Aileen set her spoon down again with over-deliberate care and held Saorla's gaze, fierce, no tears. "It's hard for me, too, you know. OK, so, I didn't give birth to them, but if I'd ever had a baby, I can't imagine I could've loved it more than I love those boys. I fretted over them in their cribs. I watched them grow up—God, I'm so proud of them both, even when they are acting the eejit. I was there that night, remember? When they were going to take Jim on?"

Saorla nodded. "I remember."

"I was afeared he'd kill yous all in a drunken rage. You've no idea what a relief it was when you left him for good, and I thought maybe…" Aileen laughed ruefully. "Maybe we'd be together at last. We both knew it couldn't be, but I kept hoping, you know? That something would change. All those times I had to bite my tongue so as I didn't beg you not to leave me—"

"It wouldn't have made a difference," Saorla said. "The boys needed their space."

Aileen nodded. "You did it for them in the end, I know, same as when you left Jim. But the reason I stayed quiet…" Aileen reached around the dessert plates and took Saorla's hands in hers. "You'd already sacrificed too much. The pain you went through when your family turned their backs on you—I never told you the Father sent the nuns round, did I?"

"The nuns? No, you did not."

"They turned up one Saturday morning. You were shopping for the boys' school uniforms, as I recall. They advised me—strongly—to encourage you to go home to Jim, where you belonged. So I told them straight. Jim Tierney is a good-for-nothing bastard. Says they, 'Don't speak of men like that. Our

Lord Jesus was a man.' Says I to them, 'Aye, and so was Judas,' and off they went, muttering and twiddling their rosaries. God only knows what tales they went back to Father Corcoran with. He gave me hell for months."

Saorla's heart landed with a heavy thud as she remembered something else that had happened back then. "That's why you left the choir. Because of me."

For the first time in years, Aileen looked like she might cry. "No, my love. Because of *all* the women. I'd look around at them hiding their black eyes behind hats and hair, or holding their arms tight to their chests, curled up so small, and all of them dead on their feet. I couldn't take it anymore, all this blaming women for men's wrongdoing."

"Father Corcoran blamed you, didn't he? For me leaving Jim."

Aileen's gaze fell to their still-joined hands. "He called me unholy and the worst kind of whore for coming between a man and his wife."

"You should've told him the truth."

"No. You'd already lost your family because of that bastard. I didn't want you thinking the Lord had abandoned you, too."

"Oh, God, Aileen. I'm so sorry." Saorla lowered her head in remorse. That Aileen had suffered for her was ripping her ragged.

"Well, I'm not." Aileen's grip on her tightened until Saorla winced.

"Steady on now, you're going to break my fingers," she warned and even managed a little laugh. Aileen eased off but didn't let go.

"Look at me, Saorla."

It took a bit of work to shake off the sadness and be sure she wouldn't bawl, but Saorla eventually looked up, and was greeted by Aileen's beautiful, smiling face.

"I'm still waiting for you, my love. And I'll wait for eternity, if that's as long as it takes."

15: MIA

SAORLA AWOKE WITH heart pounding. It took another round of hammering on their room door to realise it hadn't been a dream that had given her a fright.

"What is it?" Aileen asked sleepily. And she claimed there were no benefits to losing her hearing.

"I don't know." Saorla shuffled across to 'her' side of the vast double bed they'd fashioned, and grabbed her dressing gown from the chair.

"Is there a fire?"

More knocking, followed by, "Saorla? Aileen? Are you there?"

"That's Erin." Struggling into her dressing gown on the move, Saorla went to unlock the door. A cold sweat now joined her pounding heart; Erin sounded frantic. She looked it, too, and started talking at speed before Saorla got a word out.

"Sorry I woke you. I was going to ask if Finn's with you, but obviously, he isn't. I don't know where he's gone, or how long ago he left. I'm not sure what to do."

"All right, Erin, would you slow down for me there? What time is it?"

"Quarter past seven. I awoke fifteen minutes ago, and he wasn't in the bed, so I checked downstairs to see if he'd gone early to breakfast. The lad on the reception desk hasn't seen him."

"Neither have we."

Erin covered her face and mumbled into her hand.

"What are you saying?"

Erin moved her hand away but kept her eyes averted. "It's my fault, Saorla. I told him last night if he didn't drop the bad attitude, I was finished with him. I didn't mean it, not after he's done so well. But he was…" She cleared her throat. Colour filled her cheeks.

"He was trying it on?"

Erin nodded swiftly, embarrassed. "Aye, he was. He'd had too much to drink, and he wasn't taking no for an answer."

Saorla was horrified.

"Oh! No! He didn't try to force himself on me or anything like that. Just got in a sulk when I said I wanted to sleep."

"Erin, if my son ever—"

"No, I swear. He's not like that. God, I'm terrible sorry." She looked away, along the corridor to their room. "I'll go and have another look around. He can't have gone far." She turned back and attempted a smile. "Sorry again for disturbing you."

"Don't you be sorry. Let me know when you find him, all right? I'll be having a few choice words, worrying you like this."

"I'm overreacting, don't listen to me. I'll see you at breakfast?"

"You will," Saorla agreed. She watched Erin all the way to the stairs before she closed the door, meeting Aileen's inquisitive gaze, which changed in an instant to a smile of reassurance.

"He'll be just taking a walk."

"D'you think?"

"Well, maybe not a walk. Getting a bit of fresh air."

"Aye, maybe." Saorla wasn't so sure. It wasn't like Erin to make something of nothing, and it wasn't like Finn to be up and out so early. "I'm going for a shower, Ail."

She made it a quick one, too, because she had a feeling Erin would be back very soon. She wasn't wrong.

"He's taken my car keys."

"He's done what? Are you sure?"

"They're not where I left them."

"But he hasn't driven since…"

"His accident? I know. He told me. But the car's gone."

"Oh, Jesus. Right. Let's think." Saorla bustled back across the room. "Has he got his phone on him?"

"As far as I know, but he's not answering."

Saorla brought up Finn's number and pressed the call button.

"Let's see him ignore his mother," Aileen said confidently, but it rang on.

"What are we now?" Saorla squinted at the screen. "Gone half past. I'll give our Sean a call."

"I can't see him being up yet," Aileen asserted.

"He's got a two-year-old son."

"Aye, fair dos. Erin, would you like a cup of tea?"

"No, thanks. I..." She burst into tears.

"Oh, come on now." Aileen—still in only her nightie—put an arm around Erin and steered her over to the chair.

"He's always so nervous when he gets in the car, telling me to slow down, or stop at junctions when I don't need to. He won't cope behind the wheel."

Aileen shushed her, and looked up at Saorla, her worry evident on her face. "I'm sure he'll be fine."

"I'll knock his stupid head off," Saorla muttered.

It took Sean a few rings to answer. "Hello, Mum?"

"Good morning, darlin'. Are you all right?"

"I am. Are you?"

"I'm fine. Listen, I'm after for your brother. Is he with you, by any chance?"

"No, he's not. Should he be?"

"No idea. He left early this morning—"

"It could've been last night," Erin said.

"He left at some point in the past eight hours. He's taken Erin's car."

"Are you having a laugh?"

"Do I sound like I'm joking, Sean?"

"Sorry. I wasn't thinking. Where would he go? He doesn't know anywhere. And how's he driving with his leg? He won't—"

Saorla cut him off. "I don't know!"

"It's an automatic," Erin explained, seeing as Sean was yelling down the phone and she'd been able to hear him loud and clear.

"Well, that's good," Aileen said, as if it solved everything, and set about making cups of tea in case it didn't.

Saorla watched her in a daze, while Erin tore strips off the scrunched tissue in her hand. Sean said something.

"Sorry, what was that, darlin'?"

"I'll go out and look for him."

"May I come with you?"

"Aye, it's probably wise. See you in ten minutes."

***

"I'm calling the police."

"Sean…"

"We've covered every road, Mummy."

"Just once more back to your place. Please?"

Sean sighed and switched off his indicator. The traffic lights changed to green and he moved off.

They'd gone from the hotel into the town centre, where there was a twenty-four-hour bar, but the place was locked up, and the bookie's wasn't open yet. From there, they'd driven up and down every side road, then out to the village where Sean lived, and back into town again. There was no sign of Erin's car, nor of Finn on foot.

"It's not like I'd actually be calling the police on him," Sean reasoned. "I just planned to have a quiet word with Aitch."

"Won't he have an obligation to act on it?"

"Finn's done nothing wrong. Has he?"

Saorla didn't like Sean's tone one bit. "No, he hasn't," she answered brusquely.

Neither spoke again until Sean stopped the car outside his house and rubbed his hands over his face. Saorla refused to look at him, fearing the open contempt for his brother she'd see. A door opened a couple of houses along from Sean's, and Josh stepped through it, his eyes on Sean all the way down the path and out to the car. Sean wound down the window.

"No luck?" Josh asked. Sean shook his head. "Where have you searched?"

"Town, The Red Back Club, the bookie's, the park—I suppose he could've found his way to the beach."

"You tried the chapel, I presume?"

"Why would he go to the chapel?"

Saorla was thinking the same thing.

Josh took a step back and folded his arms.

Sean put the car in gear. "I'll try the chapel," he muttered.

"Good idea," Josh said as he turned on his heel and walked back to his house.

"What am I missing here?" Saorla asked.

"What you've said all along, Mum. We're more alike than we let on."

***

Sean left an empty space between his and Erin's car in the chapel car park. Saorla had already spotted Finn. He was sitting on a bench across from the chapel's main door, back hunched, chin resting on clasped fists.

"Looks like he's praying," she thought aloud.

"Does he still pray?"

When they were young, Finn had loved saying his prayers, and more often than not was the one to field Sean's doubtful questions. But the sad truth of it was, Saorla didn't know anymore. She wasn't sure she even knew him.

"Go talk to him, darlin'."

"Me? What am I supposed to say?"

"All that training of yours, you'll come up with something."

Sean studied Finn a moment longer and shrugged. "I'll give it a go, but don't say I didn't warn you when he knocks me out cold."

"He won't." Besides, she was there to separate them if need be. She waited for Sean to get out of the car and then followed, stopping when she was within hearing distance.

"'Bout ye?" Sean slowed as he approached his brother.

"Sean," Finn acknowledged without looking up from the spot on the ground he seemed to have taken a liking to.

Sean sat next to him. "What're you doing here?"

"Thinking." Finn leaned back, eyes unfocused. "I thought it'd be open. You know the way the church always is?"

Sean chuckled. "Has it been that long since you went?"

"Do they not stay open anymore?"

"You're asking the wrong person."

Their church still opened all day Thursday and Friday for adoration, but Saorla thought it best not to interrupt.

"They have midweek Mass here of a Wednesday," Sean said. "Or a Communion service, at least."

"Do you partake?" Finn asked.

"I'm at the hospice, usually, but I'm off this week while Mum's here. We could go together...if you like."

Finn homed in on the chapel. "It's peaceful."

"Aye, it is. I come here quite often—to think."

Finn turned his head, giving his brother a half smile. "You like it here? In England."

Sean looked around him at the lovely gardens, the trees full of young crab apples and acorns, the rainbow blooms in the well-kept flowerbeds. "It's home," he said.

"What about Mum?"

"We're grown-ups, Finn. It's time we both started acting like it."

16: Grace

"Are ye away now?" Aileen asked Erin as the five of them exited the chapel on Wednesday morning. There had been around a dozen for Holy Communion, and Father Mallick had performed the Eucharist quite acceptably, Saorla thought.

"We are," Erin said. "We need to get petrol, and then we're off to L—"

"Llandudno," Finn cut in with a sideways glance at his brother that said 'that was a close shave'. "It's in Wales, Aunty Aileen." He smiled shiftily at Saorla and then grunted and rubbed his thigh.

"She knows," Saorla said curtly. Finn was constantly in pain, but he was laying it on a bit thick, and Saorla had a good idea why. Judging by Aileen's next words, so did she.

"Don't forget to send us a postcard."

"For sure, if we can find one."

"Oh, it shouldn't be too difficult, with it being a seaside town and everything. It's a smashing wee place, too. Who needs big, smelly cities like…London…when you can have just as much fun at the seaside? I hope yous brought buckets and spades."

"I knew we'd forgotten something." Finn grinned.

Sean had his head down, but the way it was bobbing, he was clearly finding the whole conversation hilarious.

"Mrs. Tierney!"

Saorla glanced back over her shoulder to find Father Mallick striding their way. She looked at Aileen, who raised a brow. They stopped walking.

"I'll wait in the car," Sean said.

"All right, darlin'." She hoped Finn and Erin would wait, too, so she could say goodbye properly.

Father Mallick reached them and shook their hands. "Mrs. Tierney, Miss Cullen. It was lovely to see you in the chapel this morning. I didn't get a chance to speak to you on Sunday. I'd have liked to have come to the house, but I was officiating a wedding."

"On a Sunday?" Saorla asked, incredulous.

"Yes, indeed. I trust this morning's Communion was up to your standards?"

"Very sure of yourself, aren't ye?" Aileen joked, or, at least, made it sound like a joke.

"I keep to the teachings of the Roman Catholic Church as far as is possible. Dylan's baptism...trying to incorporate the parents' and guardians' various beliefs and values presented quite a challenge."

"You did a grand job, Father," Saorla assured him.

The priest bowed his head in thanks.

"So..." Aileen began in a tone Saorla recognised. She braced herself. "Did ye leave the Church for your wife?"

"Aileen!"

Father Mallick smiled. "Don't worry, Mrs. Tierney. I get asked often, and I really don't mind answering. No, I didn't. I left because I disagree with Rome's stance, that women's ordination is incompatible with Christian faith. It is not God who chooses whom to ordain. It is men. I realise, of course, this is heresy to your ears."

"Not at all," Aileen said at the same time as Saorla said, "Yes." She regarded Aileen in disapproval.

Father Mallick went on: "It is perfectly all right for you to have different views. God calls us all to worship, but He does not prescribe what form that worship should take. It's my belief it should be meaningful to each of us, individually, and for some, a formal service in a special building—" he gestured to the chapel "—has either no meaning at all or a negative one. For instance,

I lead a prayer evening for former prisoners who simply cannot engage with formal worship because of their time in borstals, secure hospitals, prison, and so on. For them, one institution is much like another. So, we meet in a pub's function room once a week, where we pray, sing hymns, some receive Communion, we read the Bible together, and we talk. It is informal, but civil, and it means a great deal to those who come along."

"That sounds very worthwhile work, Father," Saorla said. She heard an engine revving in the car park, and stepped off, as did Aileen. The priest walked with them.

"Thank you. I like to think so."

"May I ask, Father…" Aileen peered at Saorla before continuing. "What's your view on same-sex marriage?"

Saorla was in more than half a mind to run the rest of the way to Sean's car, but she forced herself to take measured steps.

"That's a very interesting question. As you know, the Bible is quite clear on this point: marriage is the joining of one man and one woman, to the exclusion of all others. However, it is only one form of relationship, and it's a matter the Church has been debating since the change in English law. As it stands, same-sex marriage is not sanctified, but we do perform blessings. The wedding on Sunday was a civil marriage with a Christian blessing."

"Here at the chapel?" Saorla asked.

"Yes," Father Mallick confirmed.

They'd reached Sean's car; Erin had manoeuvred out of the space and was waiting with the engine running.

"It's been lovely to talk to you, ladies," Father Mallick said. "Will we see you again?"

"Oh, yes!" Aileen answered indulgently. Saorla fought a smile, but it escaped anyway.

"I'd imagine so," she said.

Father Mallick laughed and shook their hands once more. "Enjoy the rest of your holiday." With a nod of acknowledgement to Sean, he was in his car and away soon after.

Finn leaned out of the passenger side window. "Mother! Are you going to come and say goodbye?"

"Oy, cheeky! Don't use that tone with me." She went over and gave his chin a pinch. "You don't fancy driving today, no?"

"I think I'll leave it to the expert."

"Very wise. When are you home? Saturday?"

"Aye, but if it's late I'll stay over at Erin's. I need to talk to you about something when I get back. It's not a bad thing."

"All right, darlin'. Let me know you're safe, won't you?"

"I will, Mum."

She stooped to give him a kiss and then moved aside for Aileen to do likewise.

"Behave yourselves, all right?" she said sternly.

"We always do!" Finn protested.

Aileen laughed and backed up next to Saorla. They watched in silence as the car moved off, waited briefly at the exit for a break in traffic, and tootled into the distance.

"Yes," Aileen said and walked to the back door of Sean's car.

Saorla replayed the morning's conversations, but couldn't pinpoint anything requiring an answer. "Yes to what?"

"If I didn't have my mum, I'd come here with you."

A lump rose in Saorla's throat. She swallowed it down and went around to the passenger door, meeting Aileen's gaze over the car's roof and trying to make sense of her answer.

Aileen shrugged. "Fifty years, my love. We've never slept in separate beds, or not in the same room. I thought I'd done something wrong."

"No, Aileen. It was on me, but I promise you, it won't happen again."

"Good." She quickly ducked out of sight, but Saorla caught a glimpse of the tears—of relief, she hoped. She climbed in beside

Sean. He smiled, watching Aileen in the rear-view mirror to make sure she'd her seat belt on before he moved off.

"Where d'you fancy going today, then?" he asked.

"Back to the hotel to freshen up," Aileen said.

Saorla pursed her lips to stop her laughter and noticed Sean do the same.

"The hotel it is," he said. He pulled out onto the road and shifted through the gears. "Don't bite my head off, all right? But shall I ask if they can move you into Finn and Erin's room?"

"Sean!" Aileen shouted from the back seat.

Saorla felt the rush of heat up her cheeks. "You heard what we were saying?"

"The windows are open, Mummy."

And so they were, which was as well. The breeze was very welcome indeed. "Aye, darlin'. Why not?"

"Are you sure now?"

Saorla turned in her seat to see behind her, the pain in her neck instantly soothed by the vision of Aileen's beguiling smile. "I'm sure."

About the Author

Debbie McGowan is an author and publisher based in a semi-rural corner of Lancashire, England. She writes character-driven, realist fiction, celebrating life, love and relationships. A working class girl, she 'ran away' to London at seventeen, was homeless, unemployed and then homeless again, interspersed with animal rights activism (all legal, honest ;)) and volunteer work as a mental health advocate. At twenty-five, she went back to college to study social science—tough with two toddlers, but they had a 'stay at home' dad, so it worked itself out. These days, the toddlers are young women (much to their chagrin), and Debbie teaches undergraduate students, writes novels and runs an independent publishing company, occasionally grabbing an hour of sleep where she can.

Social Media Links

Website: debbiemcgowan.co.uk
Newsletter Signup: eepurl.com/b8emHL
Blog: deb248211.blogspot.com
Facebook: facebook.com/DebbieMcGowanAuthor and facebook.com/beatentrackpublishing
Twitter: @writerdebmcg
YouTube: youtube.com/deb248211
Instagram: instagram/writerdebmcg
Google+: plus.google.com/+DebbieMcGowan
Tumblr: writerdebmcg.tumblr.com
LinkedIn: uk.linkedin.com/in/writerdebmcg
Goodreads: goodreads.com/DebbieMcGowan

By the Author

Checking Him Out Series
Checking Him Out (Book One)
Checking Him Out For the Holidays (Novella)
Hiding Out (Novella – Noah and Matty – HBTC Crossover)
Taking Him On (Book Two – Noah and Matty)
Checking In (Book Three)
The Making of Us (Book Four – Jesse and Leigh)

Seeds of Tyrone Series
~ co-written with Raine O'Tierney
Leaving Flowers (Book One)
Where the Grass is Greener (Book Two)
Christmas Craic and Mistletoe (Book Three)

Hiding Behind The Couch Series
The ongoing story of 'The Circle'…
Nine friends from high school;
Nine friends for life.

The Story So Far…
in chronological order:
novellas and short novels are 'stand-alone' stories, but tie in with the
series. Think Middle Earth—well, more Middle England, but with a
social conscience!

Beginnings (Novella)
Ruminations (Novel)
Class-A (Short Story)
Hiding Behind The Couch (Season One)
No Time Like The Present (Season Two)
The Harder They Fall (Season Three)

Crying in the Rain (Novel)
First Christmas (Novella)
In The Stars Part I: Capricorn–Gemini (Season Four)
Breaking Waves (Novella)
In The Stars Part II: Cancer–Sagittarius (Season Five)
A Midnight Clear (Novella)
Red Hot Christmas (Novella)
Two By Two (Season Six)
Hiding Out (Novella – CHO Crossover)
Breakfast at Cordelia's Aquarium (Short Story)
Chain of Secrets (Novella)
Those Jeffries Boys (Novel)
The WAG and The Scoundrel (Gray Fisher #1)
Reunions (Season Seven)
To Be Sure (Novella)
Tabula Rasa (Gray Fisher #2)
What A Scorcher! (Short Story)
Goth of Christmas Past (Novel)

Stand-Alone Stories
Champagne (LGBT Historical Novel)
'Time to Go' in Story Salon Big Book of Stories (Contemporary Short Story)
And The Walls Came Tumbling Down (Sci-fi Novel)
No Dice (Sci-fi Novel)
Double Six (Sci-fi Novel)
Sugar and Sawdust (M/M Romance Short Story)
Cherry Pop Valentine (M/M Romance Short Story)
Coming Up ~ co-written with Al Stewart (LGBT Short Story)
Of the Bauble (LGBT Fantasy Romance Novella)
So Long, Little Black Diamonds (Short (True) Story)
The Pastor's Last Drop (Historical Novel (Ongoing) – Wattpad)
When Skies Have Fallen (LGBT Historical Romance Novel)
A Snowy Ball (When Skies Have Fallen #1.5)
The Great Village Bun Fight (Contemporary Novella)

www.hidingbehindthecouch.com
www.debbiemcgowan.co.uk

Beaten Track Publishing

For more titles from Beaten Track Publishing,
please visit our website:

http://www.beatentrackpublishing.com

Thanks for reading!